When you pass out and come to, there's this feeling of loss. Like time has passed you by and you've somehow been cheated out of a part of your life. When I found my sister, Jessica, dead, I passed out and when I woke up, her body was gone. The blood was gone. She was gone. There was this piece missing from my mental jigsaw puzzle. A family portrait with a missing head. When I woke up on the beach that day, it was nothing like that. It wasn't like I had missed a part of my life. It was as if it had never been.

I sat up, salty and wet, coated in a fine layer of sand and pebbles and bits of dried kelp and tried to remember how I had gotten there. The ashes, the cliff, falling like Alice down the rabbit hole. I rubbed my temples in tight circles. Blood, blood, blood. Every significant moment in my life was covered in it, drenched, soaked, consumed by it. The sea still held its quiet menace, the air still hung in gray sheets, but something was different and it wasn't the scenery.

"What is wrong with me?"

As soon as the words left my throat, I could feel it. There was something different in my voice, my words, the way my tongue crept across my lips.

Books by C.M. Stunich

SHE LIES TWISTED

C.M. STUNICH

SARIAN ROYAL

She Lies Twisted
Copyright © C.M. Stunich

For information address Sarian Royal Indie Publishing, 1863 Pioneer
Pkwy. E Ste. 203, Springfield, OR 97477-3907.
www.sarianroyal.com

ISBN-10: 1938623029 (pbk.)
ISBN-13: 978-1-938623-02-8 (pbk.)

Cover art and design © Amanda Carroll and Sarian Royal
Optimus Princeps font © Manfred Klein
Stock images © Shutterstock.com

to the real Goth girls, who don't go for the popular boys at school but for dead ones on the beach with stitches in their faces

eligible for some scholarships for like orphans or whatever." I tucked a strand of my hair behind my ear. I hated that that it was so bright and cheerful and straight. I was tempted to dye it black, but it felt so cliché that I ended up just leaving it Barbie blonde.

"That's sweet," Boyd mumbled around another bite of sandwich. "But I'm still not taking your money, Neil." I ground my teeth together. *Stop being so stubborn, you stupid oaf.* I studied my best friend's massive form, hunched over the brown paper bag like a starving wolf, shaved head glinting in the fluorescent lights of the cafeteria. I would've rather gone out for lunch, but our stupid school had decided to install gates last year. And metal detectors. And security guards. It was too screwed up for words.

"I'm not saying that you *take* my money, per se," I schmoozed, reverting back to the same tactic I'd used yesterday. The one that hadn't worked. "I'm just saying that with your financial aid and your chess scholarships, I will *finance* the rest of your tuition and living expenses and that when I come and mooch off you and sleep in your bed and force you onto the couch – " I was babbling. I paused and took a breath. "You can pay me back as soon as you graduate." He had finished his food and was crumpling up the garbage, slamming one ratty combat boot on the over waxed floor next to him.

"No."

"With interest," I whined, chasing after him. One of the lunch ladies was yelling at me to clean up my tray. I ignored her. "And then you won't get stuck in this shitty town at a shitty job and – " He was storming across the cafeteria, students scrambling out of his way in fear. Boyd was scary when he was mad. "Boyd!" I screamed. Faces turned and for a moment, silence reigned over my section of the cafeteria. I threw up my hood and followed him into the hallway.

"Just stop it, Tatum," he said, using my real name. I pursed my lips. "Besides, your grandma has control over that money until you turn eighteen, not you."

"My grandma can barely remember her own name, Boyd, let alone that I exist. I'm sure we can figure out a way to get the money." I wanted Boyd to go to college. Not just for him. I wasn't that selfless but for me, too. He was my other half. My friend. My partner in crime. I loved him more than I loved the bones in my own body. He marched over to the one place that he thought I wouldn't follow, the boy's bathroom.

"Neil," he said as he gestured at the dirty urinal. "Please?" I turned away and focused on the mirror over the vanity, digging out some eyeliner and smearing it across my eyelids as the sound of liquid hitting porcelain echoed in the silence. I didn't stop until I looked like a raccoon. Just the way I liked it. At the sound of a zipper being drawn, I turned back to my friend.

"Why are you doing this to me?" I asked him, knowing that I sounded stupid and selfish and ignorant.

"Neil," Boyd said in that soft voice of his, the one where his eyes got all deep and dark and his lips went bloodless. I think he was in love with me, but I never asked; it was kind of this unspoken thing between us. "Don't do this to yourself."

"Me?" I asked as he washed his hands as quickly as was humanly possible and pushed past me. "What are you talking about? I'm not the one aspiring to be a dishwasher at Applebee's!" Boyd paused and turned back around to face me, putting one meaty hand on my left shoulder, his short black nails digging into the fabric.

"Don't torture yourself with dreams that will never happen." And then he walked away, and I let him go.

That was the biggest mistake of my life.

CHAPTER TWO

I cut the rest of my classes and wedged myself between the blue and green dumpsters in the back of the school, fishing out a box of cigarettes that Boyd had taped underneath the blue one for 'emergencies' on the last day of school last year. I stuffed my earbuds in and blasted I Am Ghost loud enough that my ears rang. They were my favorite Goth-rock band. Boyd called them post-emocore. I disagreed. I smiled as I flipped through my playlist. *You should call him and apologize. More flies with honey and all that.* I tugged the earbud out of my left ear and dialed Boyd's number from heart. I didn't keep contacts in my phone. I just didn't. I'd read some article about people and memory loss because technology remembered everything for us. All of my memories were precious. When reality sucked, memories kept me alive. Just for practice's sake, I tried to pull up an image of my mother's face and frowned when it appeared wavy and fragmented.

"Damn it," I cursed as the cigarette tumbled out of my mouth and burned me right through a hole in my patchy jeans. I hit dial as I smacked at my singed flesh with my other hand.

"Hey Neil, leave a message, love Boyd." It was his voice mail.

"You asshole," I said, trying to project a smile into my voice. I was the only one that ever called him and vice versa. We liked it that way. "Are you in class? Did you ditch? Call me back." I ended the call and sent him a text that pretty much said the same thing minus the asshole comment. I picked the cigarette up off of the ground and finished it before replacing the box and melding into the mass of students pouring out the doors.

I waited at the edge of the new gate that surrounded the school grounds, back pressed up against a tree and read snippets of *Pride and Prejudice and Zombies.*

I waited for two hours.

When I finally realized that Boyd was absolutely, definitely not going to show, I packed up ship and started the dull and uninspiring walk home. White and yellow and beige colonials cast their shadows over the crumbling sidewalk, their yards wide and green and filled with trees whose lineage could be traced back further than the little, fluffy dogs that the old ladies paraded up and down the drives on their way to bridge practice. I ignored them all and they returned the

16

I knew I had to get over there. Something wasn't right with him. *Why am I even here?*

I threw some cash down on the counter and grabbed the bag.

"You know where to find me if I'm short," I yelled back as a bag of Oreos tumbled over the edge of the paper sack and slammed into the polished white linoleum.

I ran like hell to Boyd's trailer park.

It was a long way, past the colonials, past the school, past the old cemetery, behind the hospital, under the bridge. I dropped the bag in the lap of a homeless guy who cursed me out and then started laughing and saying, "Merry fucking Christmas," over and over again. There wasn't time. I suddenly felt my heart catch in my throat. Something was wrong. I knew it the way a grizzly knows when a hunter is near her cubs. It was pure, freaking instinct. Something was wrong with my Boyd.

My best friend, a grand master at chess, and the best dungeon master a girl could ever ask for.

Nothing seemed amiss when my feet finally hit the spotty lawn in front of the yellow and white single wide. The wind rushed by like a touchy-feely relative, caressing my bare skin through the holes in my jeans and pinching my cheeks with cold. I smoothed my hands down the front of my sweatshirt and forced myself to walk to his front door. I didn't knock, just walked right in like I'd done a thousand and one times before. Only this time, it was different.

I don't know what hit me first, the smell of wet pennies or the sense of hopelessness, the idea that if my phone hadn't died, if I hadn't gone to the store, if ...

"Boyd?" My voice shook, trembled and faded into the wet, red-brown carpet. "Boyd?"

In movies, when bad things happen, people always collapse to their knees all dramatic like. That's true. My knees went so weak that the idea of holding my body up just seemed ridiculous. I collapsed, hands splashing in red. It was still lukewarm. Like if I'd been here, I might've made a difference. I reached a trembling hand out and brushed my fingers across Boyd's parted lips.

Death, that hath suck'd the honey of thy breath, Hath had no power yet upon thy beauty.

"Boyd!" This time I was screaming, I think. Or maybe I was silent. Time slowed to a crawl, ceased to matter. He had struck again, Death, and he had caught me unawares. A sob escaped my lips along with a wretch. I can't describe how badly death smells. To see your friend, your last family member, laid out like a broken doll and smelling like copper and emptied bowels ... Even though I'd seen it before, I still wasn't prepared for it.

"What the fuck?" I screeched, not caring that when I slammed my fists into the floor that blood splattered my face and neck. "You fucking idiot!"

A fly buzzed in the cracked front door, swam lazily in the air in front of my face and landed on Boyd's bloodied wrists. It takes them about a half an hour to find a body. A half a fucking hour.

"Don't you dare touch him!" I screamed, scrambling forward, knees wet with him, with Boyd, and swiped at it angrily. "Don't you dare go near him."

S creaming neighbors woke me up. Cops with grim faces and questions I couldn't answer grasped my shoulder and pulled me away. They stuffed me into the back of an ambulance before realizing that none of the blood was mine. Then they stuffed me, much less gently, into the back of a squad car. I could hear the coroner or the medical examiner or whatever she was telling the cops that she thought it was suicide.

"I can't be sure yet of course," she said to the sheriff as more cops put up shiny yellow tape and scribbled on clipboards and stared quizzically over their shoulders at me. I threw up all over my seat. I was covered in blood. The thinner patches were dry and flaky like scabs. The thicker patches were worse, sticky and runny and thick as molasses. I sobbed and collapsed onto my side.

The cops felt sorry for me and took me home, parading me up the walkway like a leper, arms stretched out as far from their bodies as they could get, hands gloved. Many of my neighbors had seen the red and blue lights and were now standing on their driveways in their blue and pink terry cloth robes, sipping martinis, and holding little, fluffy dogs.

The first cop, a dark haired man who I think was Margaret Cedar's older brother, knocked first and stepped back, coughing into his unbloodied left hand. I wanted to say, "Grandma Willa is already asleep. Once she takes her meds, she's out until dawn. Just open the fucking door and let me have some alcohol from the cupboard under the sink. Let me crawl in bed and play my music so loudly that I'll have hearing problems when I'm twenty-two. If I make it that far, that is." I said nothing.

The cops exchanged worried glances. I reached out and opened the door. It creaked forward on old hinges and swung in the brisk night air like a heavy flag.

"Tatum," began the dark haired man that was definitely Margaret Cedar's older brother. "I can't just let you go in there by yourself." I spun around quickly, tears streaking through the red spots on my face and put on my best good girl smile.

"My … my grandma is upstairs. She just … she's old … I just … " I couldn't help it. I collapsed again and the cops carried me to the pretty bedroom without really knowing what they were doing and left me alone on top of the pink floral covers.

If they came back, I don't know. My mind mercifully, mercifully lulled me into another state of not-sleep and left me there for hours.

CHAPTER FOUR

B oyd.
    I slept for a week solid and thought of nothing else.

CHAPTER FIVE

I sat at the little round table in the kitchen and listened to the snap-crackle-pop of my soggy Rice Krispies and the incessant droning of the cicadas outside the screen door. Boyd had been complaining about the brisk weather we'd been having. He'd have loved to see the way the sun reflected off of the pearly white of the vintage stove and cast bright purple shadows when it hit the earrings I was wearing. He'd given me these earrings. Another one of his thrift store finds. Boyd was good at thrifting, genius even. I paused and scooped another soggy mouthful up with my spoon. Boyd and I had opened this box of cereal together less than two weeks ago. Now he was gone and it was still here glaring at me from the porcelain china that was too fine for cereal but that I used because we had nothing else.

I let the tears wash down my face and drip into the bowl. I didn't notice and I didn't care. All that mattered was finding out what Boyd's dad had done with him. I'd made up my mind to go back to the trailer park and see that he got a proper sending off, one way or another. He would've done the same for me.

I washed my bowl and dried it in a daze, eyes glazed over, looking at but not seeing the yellow roses swaying in the fall breeze. As much as the thought of going back to the place where I'd found Boyd dead pained me, I didn't feel that I had any other choice. When my sister had died, my life had been put on pause, like I couldn't move forward until she did. When I'd seen her coffin descend into the wet ground, I'd taken a deep breath and everything and everyone around me had begun to move again. I didn't stop hurting, I'd never stop hurting, but I was able to move on, to pretend that maybe one day I'd be okay again. I'd been able to meet and befriend Boyd. Maybe if I did the same with him, I could breathe again.

"Marilyn?" A voice behind me asked. I dropped the bowl into the porcelain sink and spun around. My eyes were wide and wary; my hands shook. But it was just my Grandmother. "Marilyn, darling," she said, shuffling into the kitchen in pink house shoes and teal foam curlers. "You know that china's for guests." I sighed and ignored her, snatching my backpack from the floor. When she was like this, nothing in the world could convince her that I wasn't my mother.

"I'm going out to find Boyd," I snapped, pausing in the ornate doorway. The heavy trim weighed down on my spirit like a curse. "You remember Boyd, don't you?" I continued, eyes narrowing. He had always tried to talk to her. She had always remembered him though she had thought he was my mother's boyfriend rather than her granddaughter's friend.

"You should wear dresses more often, Marilyn," Grandma Willa said, grabbing handfuls of the broken china, blood whispering down her sun wrinkled skin and splattering against the white of the sink. She picked up a sponge and rubbed at the shards, humming some old song under her breath. "You're a woman now, you should try and act like one." I huffed angrily and left her there to bleed.

Once I had escaped the yard and Anita's wary glances, I pulled out my music and picked the saddest, most depressing songs I could find. I arranged them into a playlist in alphabetical order and cried my way to the trailer park. I hoped that Boyd's worthless father hadn't done something stupid like leave his body to the county to deal with. He'd done that to Boyd's mother, or so he'd bragged. I twisted the fabric of my sweater in anger. Boyd's dad was the lowest of the low. Whatever he'd done, it couldn't have been good. This wasn't going to be easy. If I'd had my way, I would've bought him a coffin. A big white one with a colorful shot of the Virgin Mary across the top of it. I would've ordered red roses and stuffed them in glass vases and lit a thousand candles and had a funeral for two. He would've been buried next to my grandfather in the old cemetery across the street and down the hill from the school. As things sat, the best I could hope for was that Boyd would spend the rest of his unlife in a place of my choosing, somewhere where his spirit could be free.

When I reached the trailer park, I found my body seizing with anguish. My knees locked up and I came to a stop just inside the front gate. The toes of my boots refused to cross over the line between the cracked pavement and the trampled grass. Trampled by cops, trampled by neighbors, trampled by the wheels of the stretcher that was covered with Boyd's body bag. I swallowed and closed my eyes, letting the cool breeze cut me like a knife. *Cut me, kill me, take me away.* I opened my eyes. There were things I had to do first.

I pushed the last bit of strength that I had left into my legs and took that first painful step towards the front door.

His shirt is wet.

I bit my lip and forced myself forward.

Darker than black.

I was almost there, just a few more steps.

Drenched with his blood.

I hadn't even raised my fist to knock when the door to the trailer next door burst open and The Orangutang stepped out. He hunched on the rickety metal steps that looked as if they might pop their stripped screws at any moment and send him tumbling to the cigarette strewn dirt. We stared at each other for a moment before he spat at the ground and growled at me.

"What the fuck do you want?" he snapped. My usual retorts died on my tongue, buried with Boyd along with my happiness. I turned towards him and removed my hood like a person might remove their hat out of respect. It wasn't for him, it was for Boyd.

"I just wanted – "

"You just wanted?" he snarled, stepping down from the trailer and stalking towards me, shirtless and covered in red curls from bulbous belly to flabby chest. "This – " He stabbed a finger at me. "Is all – " Poked me in the chest. "Your – " Stepped on my toes. "Fault." I didn't want to cry in front of this person. This monster. This man who called himself Boyd's father. I couldn't help it. They came pouring out. A monsoon in India couldn't have drowned my spirit any faster than my tears.

"Please." I was begging, pleading. My knees began to shake. "I just want to know where he is."

"My son is *dead* because of you and look at this," he said, gesturing at the trailer behind me. "This shit is fucked. How am I supposed to live here now? The damn carpet is covered in blood!" I blinked wet eyes back at him. "You wanna know where he is? Well, fuck you!" The Orangutan shoved me forward with both hands, knocking me to my back in the grass and stalked back to the trailer, pushing his girlfriend and neighbor, Prissy, out of the way. She waited for him to go inside and slam the door before walking over to me. Her brown eyes flicked back and forth in fear and she nibbled her bottom lip until it bled. She didn't try and help me up.

"He's at the funeral home across the street from the Lutheran Church in Solma," she said. Her eyes grew wider as Danny's screaming cut through the shredded screens on the windows and bounced around the quiet trailer park. "We're supposed to pick up his ashes tomorrow, I guess." She shuffled her feet and stepped back so that I could stand. I didn't bother to brush the debris off of my clothes, but I did put my hood back on. I felt naked without it. Exposed.

"I want them," I told her quietly. Her too-pretty-for-the-park face twitched in obvious anxiety. Prissy was a nice person. Too nice for Danny. Boyd had always said he'd felt lucky to have Priscilla next door. He'd said that since his real mom hadn't wanted him, the universe had sent him someone that did. Prissy always baked him a cupcake on Fridays with white frosting and a red B. She'd always given me one, too. Tears swelled again. I fisted my hands in my sweatshirt.

"Okay," she said simply. "I … " Her eyes looked at everything but me. "We're kind of short on rent this month what with having to pay for … to pay for Boyd's … " She began to cry. Her tiny shoulders shook and little squeals escaped her thin lips. I nodded.

"Tomorrow, same time?" I asked. Her blonde curls bounced as she nodded, face buried in her hands.

The last thing I needed to see was more sadness, so I turned away and left her there to cry.

I walked back towards the school but ended up veering down a side street and sitting under the Morona County Memorial Bridge. I had climbed through one of the holes in the chain link fencing that the city put up to keep bums away and sat with my back against a stone wall. Steel support beams loomed above me like giants and shook with the passing of cars while a murder of crows pecked at one another and flapped around, fighting for the garbage that littered the pebble strewn path.

I felt empty and full all at once. It was like there was this place in my heart where Boyd had been and when he'd died, he'd taken that piece of me with him. At the same time, all of my emotions and thoughts weighed down on my stooping shoulders, seeping into me and filling me with this unbearable sense of despair. Weighted and barren. Heavy and formless. The saddest part was, I was used to feeling like this. When Mom had died, I felt this way. Dad. Jason. Abe. Jessica.

"I have nobody," I said and jumped when my words echoed back at me. *Nobody, nobody, nobody.* The crows screamed back at me in protest.

"Not nobody," Boyd had said as he rubbed my back in little circles when I'd told him about my sister. "You've got me." I punched the chain link fence and cursed when the snipped wires sliced open the soft skin between my knuckles. Drops of blood bloomed on the gashes and swelled before leaking down the sides of my hand and splattering across the stones. I couldn't stop myself from staring, from watching the blood drain from me the way it had drained from Boyd before. *And he's not the only one. You've seen it before. Jessica's face pale and the yellow sink red and the way she draped across the toilet with her hair wet and tinged pink from the dark water that swirled like ink.*

I screamed and screamed and screamed until my voice went hoarse and the sounds of my despair played back at me from the stone walls like a curse.

I slept under the bridge that night and dreamed about Boyd and Jessica. I was back in my bedroom and they were standing over me. Jessica was smiling, but Boyd's face was wrinkled with worry. I frowned at them.

"You should've told me about your brothers," Boyd chastised as Jessica moved silently away from us. I hadn't told Boyd about them. Sometimes I tried to pretend they never existed. I glared at Jessica's back. "Neil," Boyd began glancing at my chest. I startled when I realized what he was looking at and jerked my covers up around my face to hide the fact that I was wearing the sweatshirt caked with his blood. He wouldn't call me weird. Boyd never called me weird. But he would tell me that I was living in the past and that the only way to get better was to make things better and that I should put on something else.

"Yeah?" I asked with a sneer in my voice. "Why's that? You obviously didn't care enough about me to stick around." Boyd glanced away, ashamed, and I realized with a start that I was angry at him. I was angry at them both. I looked over at Jessica again. She was staring at my taxidermy collection in horror. We might've looked the same, but after starting high school, we'd stopped sharing the same interests.

Boyd opened his mouth to say something and then paused. When I glanced back at him, I realized that something was different. Boyd had hair. I pushed away my anger and reached up, running my hands through the short, red curls. I tried to smile at him. "Where did these come from?" I asked.

"I'm dead, Neil," he said sadly and when he looked up at me, his eyes were dark. "Anything is possible now." The words were nice, but his tone was melancholy. I opened my mouth to ask what the matter was, but then decided against it. It was a stupid question to ask someone who'd just killed himself. Boyd took my hand in his and squeezed it. "You can't always trust the people you love," he said. "And Neil … " One of his shaggy brows rose to his hairline. "Don't do it. You're so good for this world, don't do it."

And then I woke up.

I stayed in my crumpled clothing, ignoring the concerned stares that Prissy gave me as she handed over a heavy cardboard box. I gave her a stack of money. I didn't know how much since I hadn't bothered to count it. I'd gone home as soon as I'd woken up and stolen it straight from Grandma Willa's purse. She always left it on the nightstand in her bedroom. It hadn't taken much to steal from her. I probably could've done it in front of her face and she wouldn't have noticed.

I had decided I was going to drive to the coast

today. Give Boyd a proper burial. It was the least I could do.

"Tate," Prissy called out as I began to walk away. I paused but didn't turn back. "Have a good life." And then I heard footsteps and the sound of a screen door slamming shut and I knew another chapter of my life was closing along with it. Tears threatened again and I dashed them away with my elbow. I didn't need this. Crying again wouldn't help Boyd's spirit. But honoring his memory would. Now all I had to do was steal a car and drive a hundred miles without a license.

Perfect.

CHAPTER SIX

Grandma Willa left her keys in a frosted glass bowl by the front door. It had been shattered a million times and glued back together because if she walked by and it wasn't there, she had a fit. I got the attachment to the bowl, it was the last gift my mother had given my grandma before she got sick, but why she had to keep it on one of those stupid decorative tables by the front door was beyond me. It was just asking to be broken. I fished the keys from the bowl and flipped through them until I found the one to the Cadillac. It was a 1998 Seville, but since my grandmother never drove it anywhere, it was still in pretty good shape. Boyd and I had borrowed it once or twice, but he'd preferred his old black truck that was such a jumble of car parts that the guy who built it,

Boyd's cousin Mac, had no idea what it had started out as. I smiled at the memory as I unlocked the door and then frowned.

There would be no more riding in Boyd's truck with the busted up speakers, no more trips to the ocean, no more homemade chili with corn chips. Nothing, nothing, nothing.

"My life is nothing," I said to myself as I climbed into the front seat of the car. "It's nothing and I am fucking nobody." More tears spilled as I buckled Boyd's ashes into the front seat next to a blue-green vase I'd stolen from the living room. It still had the dusty remains of hundred year old silk flowers in it. I snatched them out roughly and threw them into the grass beside the car before peeling out of the driveway with no seat belt and the door partially hanging open. It took me fifteen minutes to notice. I smiled at Boyd's box with my cheeks still wet. "Thanks for keeping the pigs off me." He didn't respond. I pretended he did though, pretended I heard him laugh like a biker in bar. And then I imagined a conversation where he chastised me for using slang I didn't really understand and I berated him for wearing socks with holes.

"I miss you, Boyd," I said. "And I always will."

I hate long drives. Always have. Boyd had usually been behind the wheel because, with the exception of the time he taught me how, I hated driving. I'd have rather been in the passenger seat reading a magazine or painting my nails lime green or tearing through a novel I'd read a hundred times. Boyd never cared. He let me be me and he liked me that way. Nobody else had liked me since my family had died. Nobody but Boyd.

"I hate you," I spat at him as I parked the car in the empty lot and eyed the gray sea. Then I felt guilty and apologized. I unbuckled Boyd and the vase and carried them to the edge where the grass stopped and the sky began. I paused a moment and tried to think about what I should say, if anything. I'd never been particularly religious and wasn't about to start now. Some people felt tragedy drew them closer to God or the Goddess or the Holy Spirit or whatever. It just drove me away, made me angry, made me doubt even more. No holy-whatever that was worth worshipping would do what had been done to me.

I knelt down in the grass and peeled the tape off of the box. Inside was a plastic bag filled with ashes. I pulled the bag out by its knotted top and stared at it. Last week, it had been Boyd. Today, it was dirt. I grimaced.

"I'm really gonna miss you," I said as I untied the plastic and attempted to pour Boyd's ashes into the vase. The top was so narrow that I ended up with as much on my hands and the grass as there was inside. I started to cry again. I tried not to, but there was really nobody to be strong for. It was just me and the screech of the ocean against the rocks. I shook off the ashes from my sweater, scooped as much as I could from the ground, and brushed my hands against the side of the glass. It would have to do. It wasn't perfect, but it was all I had in me.

I crushed the cardboard box and folded up the plastic bag before putting them back in the car and then approached the metal railing with the vase clutched between my hands. I stepped over the danger sign that warned tourists away from the edge until I was standing as close as I could to the sea.

"Boyd," I choked out and then paused. "Johnathan David Boyd." *Yes, that was better. That felt right.* "I, Tatum Ruby O'Neil, promise to miss you everyday for the rest of my life." I squeezed my eyes shut. "And I'll love you until the day I die."

As I released the vase into the air, as it became silhouetted against the darkening sky, I thought I felt a pressure at my back, like a warning, a familiar hand guiding me away from the edge. But when I snapped my eyes open, the sensation and the vase were gone and the cliff was crumbling beneath my feet.

I was falling.

CHAPTER SEVEN

She lies twist'd, twist'd, twist'd,
On the edge of gray cliffs mist'd.

Bruised and broken, bloodied red,
Temper'd by demons, souls of the dead.

Her eyes and lips have gone to seed,
Her twist'd body no longer breathes.

Wrong'd and ruin'd, broken down,
Our twist'd gatekeep, we have found.

CHAPTER EIGHT

When you pass out and come to, there's this feeling of loss. Like time has passed you by and you've somehow been cheated out of a part of your life. When I found my sister, Jessica, dead, I passed out and when I woke up, her body was gone. The blood was gone. She was gone. There was this piece missing from my mental jigsaw puzzle. A family portrait with a missing head. When I woke up on the beach that day, it was nothing like that. It wasn't like I had missed a part of my life. It was as if it had never been.

I sat up, salty and wet, coated in a fine layer of sand and pebbles and bits of dried kelp and tried to remember how I had gotten there. *The ashes, the cliff, falling like Alice down the rabbit hole.* I rubbed my temples in tight circles. Blood, blood, blood. Every significant moment in my life was covered in it, drenched, soaked, *consumed* by it. The sea still held its quiet menace, the air still hung in gray sheets, but something was different and it wasn't the scenery.

"What is wrong with me?"

As soon as the words left my throat, I could feel it. There was something different in my voice, my words, the way my tongue crept across my lips. I brushed my hands down the front of my sweatshirt. A huge gash sliced across the gray fabric from hip to shoulder. I dug my fingers into the rend and peeled it away from my skin. My nails met rough lines but no pain. I lifted the hem and examined my belly. Dark X's crisscrossed my pale skin in a diagonal line from the bottom of my ribcage to the top of my belly button.

Stitches.

"What the – " I picked at the black thread with one of my fingernails. It was stiff and rigid but not painful and underneath it, there was only a white scar and no wound. "How long have I been here?" The wind snatched my words in cold hands and whipped them away from me. Had I been lying here for hours? Days? *Weeks?* "Impossible." I dropped my sweater over the bizarre medical experiment my midsection had become and pushed myself to my feet. Gaping wounds didn't just disappear. Maybe I was dreaming? But no ... I shook my head and reached a hand up to my hair. Dreams didn't hurt this much. I felt around my scalp for injuries and came across another coarse line of stitches.

"This is fucked," I whispered to myself, feeling the

first surges of panic. I tried to retrace my steps but could only remember the cliff crumbling then … nothing. I squeezed my eyes shut and pressed my fists against my shuttered lids. I knelt down in the sand and let the cacophony of crashing waves and howling wind wash over me. *Pain, heat, a face with dark eyes and a sad smile, rocks, my hair brushing across my cheeks as I* … I rose from my crouch and whirled to face the staircase of cliffs behind me. One after another they stepped down from the grassy coast and dipped into the water until the smallest of the five outcroppings was mostly submerged by white foam.

"I … I fell." My lips trembled, my legs shook, and like the day I discovered Boyd's body, I found myself on my knees. "I fell, I hit the rocks, my head … " I tore my sweatshirt off and threw it in a soggy mass on the wet sand. My hip, just above my jeans, my chest, just below my breasts, both of my arms above the elbow.

More stitches.

I began to unbutton my jeans.

"I would not do that, if I were you," said a voice from behind me. I turned around in slow motion, like a heroine in a horror movie, arms crossed over my chest. A woman sat on the edge of a kelp covered rock, the navy and white spray of the sea soaking her from feathered head to taloned toe. Wings spread out behind her like a cloak, fluttering in the breeze and twitching with the same amusement that was pulling her black lips away from her teeth. "You never know who might be watching." And then her wings spread even wider, blocking out the gray sky, and she launched herself into the air. I stumbled back, expecting her to dive at me, to reach for me with those gleaming claws, but she caught a current of air and began to rise in the sky above me until she was nothing but a speck among the clouds.

I rescued my sweatshirt from the sand with quivering hands.

"I am fucking losing it," I whispered to myself, blaming the fall and the cold for what had obviously been a figment of my imagination.

I forced my shaking legs up the single trail that wound back and forth along the cliff's edge. I couldn't believe what I'd seen, but yet, when I glanced down at my wrists, there was no denying that something had happened to me.

I tried to search my brain for missing pieces that I knew weren't there. When I had seen Jessica, I had passed out. I'd forgotten. But then I'd remembered, despite my own wishes, I'd remembered every detail. The way the tips of her hair hung across her frozen face, the shiny pool of black against the white tile, the soft flannel folds of her nightgown. With my most current nightmare, there was nothing. No nagging bits of memory, no insistent pounding, no whispered, unwanted thoughts.

"Get it together, Neil," I said, feeling a surge of relief at the sight of the Seville. It sat untouched in the parking lot, just the way I had left it. I dug around in my sweater pocket for the keys. "Oh shit." They weren't there. I pulled the pockets out and checked my jeans. Nothing. "Oh shit, oh shit, oh shit." I ran back down the cliff, nearly fell off (again), and forced my quivering legs to a walk. "Please be there," I whispered to myself. "Please, please, please be there." What was I going to tell my grandma? Hell, what was I going to tell the cops? How was I even going to get home?

A glint of silver caught my eye. I sucked in a breath. That had to be them.

I jogged across the sand, ignoring the strange itch in my belly where the stitches tugged at my flesh. I reached down and plucked the key from the sand without really looking at it. The chain snagged as if it were caught on something. I tugged at it harder and then realized with a shock that it wasn't my key. This was a rusted skeleton key on an equally rusted chain and it was attached to something. Something that was groaning.

I jerked my hand away from the jostling movement that was beginning beneath the sand and stepped back. I slammed into someone, hard, and felt a cold hand clasp over my mouth. "Don't panic." The mound reared up like a tidal wave, sand splashing against my skin, while the rest fell away in wet clumps. I screamed against the waxy skin that was covering my lips as the thing turned and smiled at me. It *smiled* and it wasn't even alive and probably hadn't been for a very long time. "Stay here and I'll take care of it," the person said and dropped me to my knees. I reached my hand back to my imaginary Glock. The sand monster looked nothing short of *Dawn of the Dead* fierce and if this wasn't the beginning of a zombie apocalypse, I was seriously beginning to doubt my own sanity.

"What the fuck are you doing?" I shouted against the pull of the wind. The person with the cold hand

was really just a boy and it was no wonder he was cold, he was as soaked as I was, dressed in nothing but a ratty shirt and holey jeans. I guess it never occurred to me to wonder why he was out there on the beach in the cold and why I hadn't seen him before. I was definitely losing it. "Don't touch it!" I yelled as I forced myself into a standing position and tackled him.

The sand monster swung one massive hand in an arc where the boy had been standing. Never mind the fact that he looked like he was moving in slow motion, the creep was as big as the Hulk with fists to match. "Are you insane?" I asked as I rolled away from the tangle of limbs and finally found the boy's face. "You could've gotten – " My words dissolved on the tip of my tongue.

Stitches.

I pedaled myself backwards across the sand until my spine was curved against the base of the cliff. The sand monster had turned and was finally facing towards us, shedding debris as he moved and revealing even more of the putrescent flesh that served as his skin. The bird lady had frightened me, don't get me wrong, but this thing, this thing was just *sick*.

The boy was looking at me with an equal amount of surprise.

"You tackled me," he said and then stood up abruptly, dark eyes accusatory. "What's your problem?" My eyes however were still on the monster trudging towards us. The boy sighed and turned back towards it, face bored, his pale, stitched lips set in a thin line. He began to move forward.

"Wait!" I called. He ignored me, hand reaching

outwards. The zombie thing grinned. And then his fingers brushed its battered face and it was gone. Poof. Like it was never there. There was no light show, no burst of energy, not even a body lying in the massive footprints. I waited against the wall of rock, eyes wide, fingers twitching with shock and then I stood up and ran.

I think I got about a mile down the road before he caught up with me.

"Maybe these are yours?" he asked, holding out one pale hand in front of my face. The keys dangled from one of his slender fingers. I snatched them away and turned on my heel. The boy followed.

"Leave me alone," I said, walking faster. "I do not need this shit right now." The boy blinked at me like he didn't understand. Whatever was going on, I didn't want to know. I didn't care. He stayed silent until I reached the car.

"Give me a ride home?" he asked. I almost choked. *Did he really ask me that?* I whirled on him and opened my mouth to rant then closed it again. *God, he looks pathetic,* I thought as I studied the stitches in his bottom lip and across his pale throat. *Whatever happened to me happened to him, too.* "I – " Before I could answer, another bird woman, a white one this time, with feathers for eyebrows and yellow lips landed behind him.

"We've much to discuss," she cooed, her black eyes locked onto mine. My mind whirled with both the improbability of the situation and the fear of the unknown.

I opened the door in a hurry and skidded away from

the parking lot without looking back.

CHAPTER NINE

When I got back to the house, it was dark. *Nobody noticed you were gone.* I chased that thought down with a shot of pain. *Of course they didn't. Grandma Willa wouldn't notice if she was missing her own fucking head.* I parked the car crookedly in the driveway and stomped into the house, slamming my shoes against the entry mat more aggressively than was necessary and turned on all of the lights on the first floor. I sat down at the table and ate three bowls of cereal. Then I grabbed some scissors from the drawer next to the sink and slipped the end of one of the blades beneath my stitches. I closed my eyes and squeezed.

The thread split easily beneath the metal teeth. I snatched at the ends, tugging them from my wrist. It wasn't painful but the discomfort made me gasp, like worms crawling out of my skin. I stared at the tiny, bloodless holes. It was better than having black fishing line crisscrossing my wrist like the back of some cheap corset, but I still didn't like them. I tugged my sweatshirt over my hands and dragged my tired body down the hallway and into the lavender bathroom that smelt like potpourri and mothballs. Whatever had happened at the beach, I was going to forget. Life was hard enough without zombies and harpies and boys with stitches in their face.

I stepped in front of the mirror and frowned at the paleness of my own skin. *I look just like that boy,* I thought as I opened my mouth and checked my gums. They were pale, too. "It's the stress," I told myself as I probed my skull for the rest of the offending thread. The stitches in my head were substantially more difficult to remove and I ended up with clusters of yellow gold in the sink and across the counter top like bits of blonde snow. There was even a moment where I debated cutting it all off.

I paused.

I like your hair long, Tate, it makes you look like a princess. Jessica had told me that, back when we'd still gotten along, before she'd started fucking boys I didn't know and locking me out of her room at night. I put the scissors on the counter and flushed the black thread down the toilet before heading upstairs to my room.

I begged sleep to take me, but it refused, dancing at the edges of my brain and leaving me restless and more emotional than ever. The cold eyes of the dead crows glared at me from their perch on my windowsill and the antique clock on my dresser ticked pass the useless, unwanted seconds of my miserable life. I turned onto my side and watched my reflection in the mirror. I was a mess, in more ways than one. My hair was ratty and tangled and my eyes shone with unshed tears. I was still wearing the same set of clothes that I had changed into after removing the ones soaked with Boyd's blood over a week ago. They were crusted with sand and salt and stank like the sea. I tore them off in a rage and threw them to the floor until I was standing naked in front of the oval mirror.

"Why am I even here?" I asked myself, hands grasping the faded white paint of the frame. "To suffer? I should just kill myself." But I knew as soon as I said it that I wouldn't do it. I was a coward. Unlike Jessica, unlike Boyd, they had wanted something and they'd taken it. I didn't even have the heart to do that. I collapsed to the floor in a heap and crawled over to the stack of clothes I'd been wearing the day Boyd died. I hadn't had the heart to wash them yet. I pulled my hoodie to my face and breathed in the iron scent of blood. "I'm sorry," I sobbed as I let the emotions of anger, guilt, and sadness wash over me like a tide.

Boyd is dead because you weren't good enough. Your friendship wasn't enough to keep him here. This is your fault.

"Murderer," I whispered to my reflection. Shafts of moonlight cut my face into stripes. I picked up one of my combat boots and used the heavy heel to smash the fragile, old glass into pieces.

I fell asleep on the floor, curled around the

sweatshirt, and dreamed of demons.

The next morning, I decided that I needed a taste of normalcy, of routine. So I took a shower, put on fresh clothes, and went to school. The walk was what nearly turned me around in my tracks. There was too much time to think, to wonder, about Boyd's death, the beach, everything. I turned my headphones to a song I didn't like and tried to memorize the words. Before I knew it, the gates of the school were welcoming me back to a life I felt like I'd already outgrown. I waded through the gossip and the he-said, she-said until I found myself standing outside of my first period class.

When I saw Margaret Cedar sitting in my seat, twirling her extensions around her finger, I knew the day was only going to go from bad to worse. I made myself walk in and sit down in the back row next to a kid I didn't know. I think his name was Jack or Charlie or something like that. He was fat enough to take up two desks, but I squeezed in next to him and pretended I didn't notice. His attempts at conversation were a welcome reprieve from my suffering. Everybody else ignored me which was nice and nobody had written anything new on my locker, so for a while there, I almost considered myself blessed. Then third period English rolled around and I found myself in a class of jocks and cheerleaders, kids who had either failed to get into AP English or didn't care. I was of the latter and found myself regretting it. The college obsessed AP kids were at least quiet. The ones in this class never shut the hell up.

"Alright guys, let's settle down," Mr. Summers pretended to shout over the din. In reality, he cared as little as they did. He was tenured, he was retiring at the end of the school year, why should he give a shit? "Pass your homework to the front of the room and we'll get started on our next unit." Chalk scraped across the board as Mr. Summers wrote out a sentence in his teeny, tiny handwriting. I squinted to see. Snickers resounded behind me like a chorus of chipmunks. *Chitter, chitter, chitter.*

"I hope it's Romeo and Juliet … Wouldn't that be perfect? Just like Boyd and Tate. Wonder when she'll cut *her* wrists." It was Jarrod, Margaret's boyfriend, who wasn't even a jock, just a loser. I didn't blink back tears or yell out, "What did you say?" I just turned around and spit in his face. "You fucking bitch," Jarrod shouted as we both rocketed out of our chairs. He pulled his fist back.

"Hit her, hit the stupid bitch!" It was Margaret Cedar.

"What is going on here?" Mr. Summers hadn't even had a chance to process what was happening when I swung first. My fist connected, white hot pain racking my knuckles and sending Jarrod stumbling back, blood streaming from his split lip.

"You fucking whore!" he screeched. I didn't hear, I didn't stop to see what Mr. Summers would do, just ran with my heart on my sleeve, fat tears mixing with my eyeliner and dripping down my face, thick and runny

like blood.

I sat in the park for hours, in the spot where Boyd had taught me how to play chess.

"You see this one, here?" he'd asked, pointing to a knight.

"You mean the little horsey guy?" I'd asked and watched as he'd thrown back his head and laughed, loud and raucous and passionate. I knew then that we'd be friends. We were just too perfect together.

I kept my sweatshirt wrapped around my knees, arms locked together tightly as I stared at the people passing by. Smiling people, happy people, people with friends and family. I ignored the drying blood on my knuckles and only vaguely thought to wonder if an asshole like Jarrod had any diseases.

"Why do you even bother?" a voice asked. At first I thought it was mine since I had been having that very same thought when I realized the words hadn't come from my mouth. The boy from the beach stepped out from behind the tree. He was even sadder in the perfect daylight than he'd been in the dusky evening. His head was stitched to his neck with the same black thread that I'd pulled from my skin the night before. I adjusted my sleeves. It hadn't grown back. Some part of me had said that it would. I stabbed at the holes with my nails.

"Even bother what?" I asked as he knelt down in

the grass next to me. People were starting to stare, not that I really cared, but how did he ever make it around town like that? Maybe the frosty lips and the navy eyes would work on Halloween, but as it stood, even I thought they were a bit creepy. The boy folded his legs beneath him like he expected to sit a long time. I stood up.

"Where are you going?" he asked. *I have no fucking clue*, I thought, *since I'm probably suspended.* I sat back down. He made a daisy chain while we sat in silence together. When he was finished, he handed it to me. I waved him away.

"Aren't you going to tell me what that thing was last night or are you really gonna make me ask?" The boy put the chain around his own wrist and secured it. I shuddered. The happy daisies emphasized the pale translucence of his skin and made the black cross hatches of his own stitches even more macabre.

"I meant, why do you even bother going to school anymore?" I pursed my lips. So he knew who I was. That explained the getup and the stitches. It was all a setup. Of course it was. It had to be. It was just my luck.

"So you know about Boyd, huh? Is that why you followed me to the beach? To harass me? To watch me cry?" I could feel my blood pounding in my ears. The boy blinked. I stood up again. "You could've killed me, pushing me off of that cliff and the stitches … " I paused. The more I broke down last night's events in my head, the less sense they made. I decided to keep my rant going anyway. I did best riding my anger hot. If I let it cool down, it was likely that I would never act and the boy and his friends, whoever the fuck they were, would get away with it. "You better be prepared to fucking explain yourself. You stuck a needle in my goddamn skin," I huffed, pointing a finger at myself. "And that costume, that sand guy, was that shit from the props department?" The boy opened his mouth, but I stopped him with another torrent of harsh words. "You know what, you know fucking what," I breathed. "I don't care. I don't fucking care." Tears were falling again and it was all that I could do not to break down. "I just lost the best friend that I'll ever have. He was everything to me," I shrieked through clenched teeth. "They all were and now they're all fucking *dead.*" I dropped my hands to my sides. "You don't need to go out of your way to fuck with me, okay? I'm already screwed up enough as it is." The guy had yet to speak, to defend himself, but at least he hadn't laughed. I think if he had I might've hit him harder than I'd hit Jarrod.

"I lost someone, too," was all that he said and then he was back to picking daisies again. "I'm sorry. I didn't mean to stir up any raw feelings, I just thought you knew."

"Thought I knew what?" I snapped, crossing my arms over my chest. I was starting to feel stupid now. The boy placed his newest creation atop his messy head of gray-brown hair.

"There are two cops coming down the walkway behind you." I cast a disinterested glance over my right shoulder. Sure enough it was Margaret Cedar's older brother and the school cop. I threw my hood up to cover my hair.

"Thanks," I said as I stepped around the base of the tree and out of their line of sight. The boy stood up and followed me.

"My name is James," he said, holding out a hand. I ignored him and kept walking. "You see that?" he asked as he pointed his finger across the park. I glanced up and then froze.

It was the black bird lady from the beach.

I ducked my head and began to walk faster.

"That's enough," I hissed as I slipped through a break in the hedge and a hole in the neighboring chain link fence. "I told you to fuck off, leave me alone." He kept following.

"You don't know anything do you?" he asked, this time with a touch of amusement in his voice. I proceeded down a cobblestone pathway that lead to a duck pond and a series of trails that would ultimately end up with me in my own backyard. When I reached the cover of the trees, I turned around and shoved 'James' or whoever the hell he was in the chest.

"I said fuck off!" And then I was turning around and running until my breath caught in my chest and I was standing at the edge of our fence debating the merits of actually going in. I didn't have anywhere else to go. I didn't have any money on me. What were my options? *Boyd's. Go to Boyd's.* My unconscious mind had yet to accept what my conscious one had already drowned in. Boyd was dead and gone.

Boyd killed himself and he's never coming back.

The wind whispered these words in my ears, but still, I went. I walked that familiar route and climbed in the trailer through a back window. The house smelt like bleach and new carpet, but under all that, there was just a little of Boyd. I curled up in the corner of the kitchen and hoped the Orangutan hadn't moved back in yet. I wasn't in there more than five minutes when I heard noises from Boyd's bedroom.

They're cleaning his stuff out, throwing it all away.

I rose to my feet without thinking. All I knew was that it had to stop. I had to stop them from touching it because if they touched it, if they took his flannel night shirts away, if they took the manga, if they took the ships in bottles, then Boyd would really be gone.

I flew around the corner, my hands grasping the edges of the door frame and prepared myself for a fight with the Orangutan. Instead, I found something else. Something I had been trying to prepare myself never to see again.

It was Boyd.

My insides burst open like a piñata. There it was, all of me to see, my emotions strewn across the floor like candy.

"Boyd?" The word was wet with tears. It dripped from my lips and splashed into the silence that loomed between us. Boyd glanced back at me and rubbed a hand over his beard.

"Which do you like better," he began, holding up two CDs. "Moonlight Sonata or Für Elise?" I stared at him a moment and watched him shimmer like a reflection in a glass, wobbly and unstable. He wasn't real, but now I knew I'd finally plunged over the deep end. I'd left the dock of sanity at the trailer door. But at least if I was crazy, I could have Boyd back in a way. Maybe I could even summon up my mother or Jessica or my brother, Abe? I lunged towards him.

Arms wrapped around my chest, pulled me back, and threw me to the floor in the hallway.

"Don't touch him!" James screamed, his chest heaving as he struggled to hold me back. "He isn't finished yet. If he was finished, they would call for you!" I stared at him for a long while, wondering which us was crazier. I decided I didn't care and threw him off of me. Boyd's room wasn't very big and I was at his side in three short strides.

"Boyd?" My fingers brushed his sweater, my hand reached for his face. His lips twisted, curled, became black and brittle like charcoal and began to flake across my skin. He wrapped his hand around my waist while talons, dark and gleaming, pierced into my side. I started to scream, but then he was tossing me like a doll across the room. I burst through the cheap prefab walls and into the living room. In the very spot I'd seen Boyd dead, I was now lying in danger of bleeding to death.

I lifted my sweater and stared in horror at the red liquid leaking across my hands. Boyd – or whatever it was that he'd become – crawled through the hole I'd made and came tearing after me. His back was twisted, his vertebrae exaggerated and sharp, and his eyes, like two pieces of broken glass, reflected my pale face back at me. "What are you doing?" I whispered as his talons tore through the new carpeting and reached out for my face. "Why?"

James stepped in front of me and placed a hand on the Boyd-thing's bulging forehead. In an instant, Boyd was back to normal, grinning and thrusting a piece of paper under my nose.

"You are not gonna believe this, Neil." I saw my own hand reach out and grab the paper.

"Hey!" I heard myself say. "You passed! I can't believe it!" I watched as a mirror image of myself ran forward and threw her arms around Boyd's neck. "I told you that you were smart. Stupidity skips a generation." The ghost-me withdrew and planted her hands on her hips. "It's true." Boyd ruffled my hair. "We learned that in AP Bio last week," the other me said as she knocked his hand aside. I turned my face away and stared at the dark pool on the floor. My fingers shook as I reached for the wounds in my side. *It's true, it's all true. Your life really does flash before your eyes.*

"You must've been really important to him," James said as he turned around and stared down at me, the corners of his eyes crinkling in concern. "If he's already gotten this far after what, a week?" There was still blood, lots of it, but when I touched my skin, I met roughness instead of pain. I wiped my skin off with the edge of my shirt and sat up. There were new stitches across my body from the new wounds to the old ones. I was right, they had grown back! *This isn't happening.*

I stood up.

James had turned back around and was watching Boyd brush hair away from my face. I hated when he'd done that. It had always made me feel guilty for not loving him like that.

"What the fuck is happening to me?" I asked as James continued to watch what was probably one of the most important days in my life unfold like a blurry watercolor painting right in front of what was apparently *both* of our eyes. "Why can you see that? What's going on?" James knew. He had to know. He had stitches, too. He glanced back at me.

"I was going to explain, but you took off before I had a chance." I watched my hands glide down the arms of Boyd's sweatshirt. *This is why he died. You killed him. It's because of this day that he's dead.* I closed my eyes and hoped that wasn't true.

"Can we go now?" I asked. "I think I'm going to be sick." I stumbled towards the front door and then thought the better of it before returning back to the window I'm come through in the first place.

"We can't go," James said as he glanced around. "Who's going to clean all of this up?"

"Who the fuck cares?" I snapped as I forced my bottom half through the narrow opening. The ghost Boyd and I were walking back towards his room. I had to get out of there. My feet hit the grass with a thump. I turned around to make sure nobody had heard the commotion. If they had, they were ignoring it. True trailer park style. James hit the ground behind me.

"Your blood is everywhere and there's a lot of it. Whoever finds that mess is going to think someone died in there."

"Somebody already did," I said and took off at an uncomfortably quick pace. After just a couple of minutes, my breath was growing ragged and my head was on fire. James caught up to me and stayed silent until I finally slowed.

"It may have healed up, but that doesn't mean it

won't affect you." I ignored him. If he was going to keep speaking cryptically like that, we might as well play charades. I waited until we were deep enough into the trees that it was unlikely that anyone would stumble onto us and then proceeded to have a panic attack. My emotions dragged more wet from my tired eyes than I'd ever thought possible. I dropped my face into my hands and sobbed.

"Why?" I asked as James situated himself beside me. "It was already hard enough and then I had to see him again? Why?" It wasn't really directed at him, but he answered anyway.

"It's always like that," James began as he adjusted the dirty brown laces on his gray sneakers. "You always see the person that started it. If you didn't, you'd never really understand why you were still here." I lifted my head and stared at him. I must've looked pretty pathetic because he put his arm around my shoulder and drew me closer. A sense of camaraderie passed between us. Loss. He felt it, too. I wasn't the only one. I wiped my bloody sleeve across my eyes.

"Who are you?" I asked. It was the one question I needed an answer to first. Before I opened another door and let someone else in, I had to know.

"My name is James," he said, his dark eyes clouding over with emotion. "And I died over a year ago."

CHAPTER TEN

"Step, two, three. Now, walk, two, three. Clasp your partner's hand, ladies, this is no square dancing class!" I pressed my hands over my ears and tried to weave my way between the twirling couples in Ms. Katy Meredith's over sixty-five tango class. They, of course, weren't listening to her, but to her replacement, a Mrs. Sherry Parks who, in my opinion, lacked the fire and conviction of Ms. Meredith. I nearly bumped into a couple in matching Hawaiian shirts and began to apologize when I realized they weren't actually in the class anymore, just a figment of Ms. Meredith's memories. I shook myself and kept going. James waved encouragement from behind the glass in the visitor's hallway.

Katy ignored me as I reached for her sleeve. I

faltered and saw James frown. He had assured me that it would be different this time, that she was ready. The sandman and … I paused and took a deep breath. Thinking his name wouldn't change anything. Still, I couldn't bring myself to do it. The sandman hadn't been ready. Katy was. James said it was the bird lady's job to tell and not mine. I bit my lip.

My fingers brushed the soft fabric of her shirt and slid around her delicate wrist. Ms. Meredith smiled.

"The lobby is down the hall," she said, her slim brows arched. "I think you're just a few decades early for this class." And then she was gone and so were half of the couples that had been dancing around the wooden floor. I breathed a sigh of relief and turned around to find Mrs. Parks eyeing me with suspicion. I covered my hair with my hood and raced back the way I had come. James was waiting at the exit for me.

"That was good," he blurted, excitement adding color to his pale cheeks. People watched us walk down the hall with either confusion, embarrassment, or downright scorn. A couple of teens, a couple of freaks. I could've sworn I heard someone say, "I hope they outgrow that someday." James couldn't help that he looked like an extra in a zombie movie. I mean, the new clothes and the shower had helped, but still, he looked like he needed a visit to the emergency room. I, on the other hand, had always looked this way. I flipped off a couple of yuppies in pastel sweaters. James grasped my hand by the wrist. "Don't draw attention," he said as he ushered me out the front doors of the Solma Valley Recreation Center.

"Why not?" I snapped, fumbling around in my

pocket for the last of the cigarettes Boyd had given me. I guess I was going to have to quit. Without Boyd to buy them for me ... I shook my head to clear it of memories. James frowned but said nothing. Lucky him. I wasn't in the mood for it. "So," I asked as we paused at the curb and waited for a break in the traffic. "You never told me how long I have to play 'grim reaper' for." I emphasized the words with my fingers. James shook his head.

"Technically," he said as we began to cross the street. "I'm the grim reaper. You're the summoner." I snorted and stuffed the cigarette between my lips.

"Look, I like a game of Dungeons and Dragons as much as the next girl but come the fuck on." I was starting to lose my patience. I had been weak yesterday, broken, twisted inside. I had let James put his foot in the door because I needed a friend, but I could only handle so much. Something weird was going on, true, but summoner? Really? "If you keep up with this crap I might have to kick you out of my house." James' face dropped. He'd been homeless for almost a year. Not a good joke. I thought about apologizing but realized I didn't have a light for my cigarette. It pissed me off enough to keep quiet.

You see, when someone you love dies, everyone tries to pretend like there's this huge, yawning gap that you spend everyday of your life standing at the precipice of, trying not to fall in. But really, it's a series of smaller gaps, little things that hurt the most. Boyd had always been my light, in more ways than one. I threw the cigarette to the pavement.

"Now what?" I asked. "Do I get a gold star or

something?" James chuckled. At least he thought I was funny.

"We find another harpy and get our next assignment." I spit at the ground.

"Why?" James' face twisted in pain and he glanced away.

"I don't know." I threw up my hands and began to walk away from him. He caught up to me. "Because if we don't, somebody's loved ones will be trapped in purgatory." James wrapped his cold, skinny fingers around my wrist. "If you don't send them to the Akashic Library, they're nothing more than ghosts." I tried to pull away. "*Forever.*" I sighed.

"Will I have to see him again?" I asked. Truthfully, when I'd snuck out last night to retrieve the cigarettes I'd left taped under the school dumpster, I'd also gone back to the trailer. Luckily, the Orangutan hadn't come home and found the destruction yet; everything was as we'd left it. I'd sat on the kitchen floor and cried while I'd watched Boyd and I bake cookies and stick mini M&M's on the tops. What I'd meant was, will I have to send Boyd to his next life? Will I have to touch his arm and watch him smile at me and then see him disappear from existence forever? Poof. Gone. My Boyd. My best friend. I sucked in a harsh breath.

"Yes." James chose not to elaborate. Simple seemed to work better for him. Last night, I'd barely gotten any information from him at all. The only things I knew were these: James and I were both dead yet somehow *not* at the same time; the bird ladies (there were men, too) were harpies that guided us to souls that needed help; and when I touched a person's ghost or spirit or whatever you wanted to call it, it either went to the Akashic Library (still no clue where or what that was), or it turned into a demon like the sandman, like Boyd. I sighed.

"Let's go to Denny's," I said abruptly and turned in the opposite direction. When I looked back, James had frozen in place and was staring at something across the street. I followed his gaze. Movement flashed down an alleyway like a shooting star. I blinked and it was gone. "What the hell?" James grabbed my arm and forced a smile.

"I haven't been to Denny's in like, forever." He tugged me away from the alley and down the street. I let him drag me several blocks before extracting myself from his grasp.

"I'm guessing you're not going to explain that to me either?"

"If you buy me a breakfast special, I might feel obligated to reveal the truth." James flashed his hands in front of his face. He was pretending to be happy, to joke around, but even though I'd just met him, I could tell that whatever we'd just seen in the alley was bothering him. I let it go for the time being. We both needed an endless cup of coffee and a stack of pancakes. I'd stolen another twenty from Grandma Willa's purse before we'd left and James hadn't had a job in over a year, so I guessed it'd be my treat. James had barely eaten since he'd died. He'd told me plenty about *that* when I'd let him raid my cupboards last night.

"So," I asked as we passed through the dirty glass of the front door and seated ourselves in a corner booth. "Can we like, starve to death or are we, uh, I dunno, immortal or something?" James shrugged as he pulled out a pair of menus from behind the napkins and handed one to me.

"When I asked Ehferea that, she told me we were *indefinite*." He pitched his voice to match the low, melodic tones of the black harpy lady. I opened my menu but didn't look at it. I knew what I wanted.

"*Indefinite?*" I mimicked back at him. "What the fuck does that mean?" James buried his face in his menu like it was of the utmost importance and ignored my question. I tapped my nails on the Formica tabletop and studied the chipped purple nail polish.

"You know," he said after what seemed like forever. "Subject to no limitation or external determination, immeasurably or inconceivably great or extensive, endless." He closed his menu and grabbed mine, stuffing them both back behind the condiments. I frowned at him.

"You sound like a dictionary." He grinned.

"*Merriam-Webster*," he said. I rolled my eyes and leaned forward, voice pitched in a menacing whisper.

"I know what it *means*," I said, putting all of the frustration and confusion I was feeling into my voice. "But what does it *mean*." The waitress approached us warily before we could finish and took our orders. She didn't look happy about it. I decided to leave her a big tip. It would teach her not to stereotype.

"It means," James said, his face droopy. "That we're here until whoever it was that decided we weren't ready to pass on changes their mind. It could be today, it could be next week, it might be never." I sat back up, my spine stiff with fear. Forever? That was a long time to suffer alone. I sucked in a deep breath.

"Okay," I replied carefully, trying to figure out which of my hundred questions I was going to ask next. "But why?" James smiled, but it seemed forced, stretchy and pliable like rubber, like I could turn it back into a frown at any moment.

"I told you," he said. "To help people."

"But why?!" I slammed my hands on the tabletop, eliciting stares. I tugged my hood closer around my face and lowered my voice. "Why us? Why not someone else? Why not the harpies?"

"They can't," he said simply. He put on a real smile for the waitress and thanked her for our drinks. I tugged my soda against my chest and jammed the straw against the roof of my mouth.

"Why?" James sighed.

"Maybe you should talk to Ehferea or Nethel. It helped me a lot when I first started." I shook my head. I wasn't ready to talk one on one with the harpies. Not yet. "They're not from here," James said as he stroked his finger down the side of the plastic cup.

"Not from where?" I asked as my skin broke out in goose bumps. I wasn't going to like this.

"From," James paused and took a shaky breath. His skinny chest rattled like he had a pneumonia. I thought about offering him my sweatshirt. "You know, like, earth." I sighed and leaned my head on my arm. James stayed quiet until I lifted my eyes to meet his.

"Go on," I moaned and sucked down half of my Coke in one sip. Too bad it didn't have any rum in it. I could've used some alcohol, but I'd drank it all the week Boyd died and I had no way to get more.

"Well," James began and sucked on his lower lip, his tongue playing across the bumps of his stitches. "They're from a place called the Akashic Library." I stopped him right there.

"Okay, you keep talking about this library and how it's so fucking important for souls or spirits or whatever to go there. Why? What is it? How could these harpies be from there? Isn't it just for dead people?" James shook his head.

"Technically, it's just on another plane of existence. Anyone could go there, if they knew how." I stared at him. He had just said 'another plane of existence' like I'd say New York. Yeah, it was far away, but if you had the money for a plane ticket …

All I said was, "Fantastic." We waited for our food in silence.

When the waitress finally arrived with our plates, James dug in like he was starving, finishing his entire stack of pancakes before I could eat a single slice of bacon. "So," he began, polishing off his scrambled eggs. "Tell me about yourself." I stared at him like he was crazy. I had decided I would let him in, make friends, but I wasn't sure if I was really ready. I found myself wanting to make sure he never knew anything about me. *He'll just kill himself if he finds out who you are.* I shook my head. Negative thoughts like that would get me nowhere, but I couldn't seem to help myself. Rainbows and sunshine seemed a long way away from the perpetually rainy day I seemed to be having.

When I didn't answer, he began to babble. "Well, I

guess I'll start then since we're going to be working together for awhile." I continued to pick at my food. "My name is James Douglas Campbell." He wrinkled his nose. "It doesn't really flow, I know, but my mom's last name was Campbell and my dad was a bastard. Douglas was my uncle, but I never met him since he died before I was born." James took a breath and waited, like he was expecting me to jump in at any moment and tell him that Tatum was really my name, not Neil. That O'Neil was my dad's last name because my mom wasn't much of a feminist and that I hated the taste of warm Skittles and would only eat them frozen. "My best friend's name was Sydney Bradford and she," I glanced up sharply. There it was. The sound that had convinced me last night that James could be trusted. Loss. Pain. Hurt. "She got hit by a car and died right in front my eyes and I ... " James laid his fork next to his nearly empty plate. "I drove off a bridge in the middle of winter. It was kind of an accident but not really. I wanted to die." I choked on my own breath. In his eyes, I saw myself. I saw him grasping for a reason to go on, anything to take the emptiness away. I reached my hand out, unsure if I should say something or remain silent. He looked away for a moment and when he glanced back at me, his eyes were shimmering with the barest hint of unshed tears.

"I am totally, crazily, obsessively into xylography, I hate reality shows, and I play the harmonica." James held up his arms with a smile. "There!" he said, sighing and sagging against the back of his seat. "Now you know everything about me. Your turn." I smiled.

"You would've loved my sister," I said as I dug into

my food with renewed fervor. "She always wanted to date a boy who would play the harmonica for her."

Misery loves company.

After dinner, James and I walked back to the house. I had decided to let him stay there while we got this whole 'indefinite' grim reaper thing sorted out. He had no where else to go and I needed information. For the moment, it was a win-win situation. I was actually starting to feel some of the fog from Boyd's death melting away when I turned the corner onto my street and saw that all of the lights were on. It was weird to see any lights on in our house after seven. Grandma Willa liked to check in early and sleep late. I picked up the pace and motioned for James to hurry up.

Grandma Willa was standing in the front yard in one of those old fashioned night gowns that old people in the South like to wear. It looked like a white canvas sack to me, but I was sure that fashion was the last thing on her mind. If she still had one that is.

"Shoo!" She was shouting, flicking her hands at one of the trees that lined the edge of the front yard. "Go on, get out of here!" I put a hand to my forehead and turned to James.

"Go ahead and go inside. Wait in the downstairs bedroom for me." He nodded but didn't move. I raised my eyebrows at him. The neighbors were starting to come out of their houses to stare. It was time to defuse the situation or deal with social services again. The last thing I needed was for some snot nosed social worker to try and place me with the state. James began to drag his feet towards the front door. I decided that was as good as I was going to get and walked up to my grandmother. I placed my hands on her tiny shoulders and leaned down.

"Come on, Mom, let's go back inside and I'll make you some tea." Grandma Willa always responded better when I called her Mom. She thought I was my mother anyway and if I played into it, it just made things that much easier. She ignored me and bent down to pick up a rock. I looked up as she tossed it at a bunch of quivering leaves near the top of the tree. Bright colors flashed as something skittered down the trunk and disappeared into the bushes on the opposite side. My spine twinged in warning.

"Watch out!" It was James. I ducked, taking Grandma Willa with me. A burst of red exploded above our heads and smashed into the tree. Bits of bark burst out at us like shots.

"No dogs in the yard!" Grandma Willa screamed as she attempted to rise. I pushed her back down and stood. The red blur skidded to a stop in some of Anita's prized begonias. I swallowed a lump of fear and tried to ascertain exactly what it was that I was looking at. It was no bigger than a coyote and bore a striking resemblance to something I'd seen in Final Fantasy VII.

"What the hell?" The words had barely left my mouth when the dog-cat thing turned and started down the brick walkway towards James. Tails like whips (I think I counted *six*) slashed through the hedges on either side as the animal bore down on James. He paused briefly before turning back towards the house and slamming the door in the thing's face. I didn't blame him. It *was* scary, but after crashing into the door and nearly taking it off the hinges, it turned around and came at me. Grandma Willa was still screaming and pointing and if I'd been a passerby, I would've sworn we were having a block party. Every house in the neighborhood was gawking from doorways and second story balconies, standing on their lawns and restraining their ridiculous dogs. They seemed concerned but not scared.

They can't see it! I realized as I moved to stand in front of Grandma Willa. But I had no delusions that it wasn't really there. I had seen firsthand what one of these things could do. But why didn't James just touch it and send it back like he'd done before? I shoved my grandmother out of the way and rolled just in time to miss the rows of double teeth and claws. The time for thinking was past, it was time to act. I searched around the grass frantically. I needed a tree branch, one of Anita's shovels, anything really. I was afraid to see what the creature would do to me if all I had to fend it off with were my bare hands.

A whistle broke across the night.

The monster's triangular ears swiveled back. It paused in the slow, stalking circle it had been pacing around me and twisted its neck 180 degrees back to look at James. He was standing in the doorway of the house with a fire poker clutched in his skinny hands.

"You have to touch it!" James screamed as the thing

shook its red fur and started to pick up speed for another charge. At least it was easily distracted.

"Touch it?" I was confused. That was James' job, right?

"Just trust me!" James yelled as he pulled his arms back like he was preparing for a grand slam. "I'll explain later!" His voice was starting to shake as the dog trotted closer. I shook myself and pulled my hood up. It was like putting on a helmet. It made me feel stronger. I started to run through the grass. The creature turned around again, almost lazily this time. It had started with such fervor. *Maybe it's getting bored?* I thought as I paused and waited for it to charge me again.

"Two fingers," James said and touched his forehead between his eyebrows. "The third eye." I held out a shaking hand. The dog monster grinned. It *grinned* just like the sandman had. It was horrid and twisted and it made my stomach hurt. I faltered. Flanks bunched, muscles contracted. It was coming straight for my face.

James screamed something I couldn't hear and I cowered back, arms over my head. A thought crossed my mind that I wouldn't die but that this was going to *hurt* and then I heard a sharp yelp and glanced up. The animal was lying on its side in the grass, a glowing arrow protruding from its side. The light around the arrow pulsed like a heartbeat while the creature lifted up its head and licked the blood streaming from the wound. For a moment, I was reminded of a German shepherd licking its side. I almost felt sorry for it.

Grandma Willa walked barefoot through the grass

and paused next to me. She balanced on her toes and kissed my cheek. "Good girl, Marilyn," she said and started limping back towards the house. Blue and red flickered across the white of the shudders and I felt my breath catch in my throat.

Cops.

James turned around and slid the fire poker under the welcome mat before standing up and pulling up his own hood. *What will they say about the stitches?* I wondered. *What about the front door? How much can they see?*

I turned around and came face to face with Margaret Cedar's brother. For the life of me, I couldn't remember his name. The neighbors continued to gawk as he glanced around the yard with a glint of suspicion in his gaze. I risked a look over my shoulder. The dog monster was panting heavily, thick streams of drool dripping across its paws as blood drained from its body and pooled on the dirt under the roses. I almost screamed when a figure stepped out from the shadows.

It was one of the harpies. I couldn't remember their names, but I recognized her as the black one I'd met at the beach. She smiled at me. I turned back around and tried not to let my hands shake.

"We've received a call about a domestic disturbance," Mr. Cedar said as he cast a disapproving glance at his partner. The other cop, who I didn't recognize, was still sitting in the passenger seat of the car doing something on his phone. It looked like he was texting. "And don't even get me started on how much trouble you're in at school."

"No, no," I said as I gestured at James to join us.

He kept his head low and dragged his feet down the walkway like he was feeling put out by having to do it. I hoped he was acting, or I was going to have to remember to be pissed off at him later. Mr. Cedar, whose name tag said Brandon, leaned down to look at James' face.

"Lord boy," he exclaimed pulling back. "What have you done to your face?" I pulled the sleeve of my sweatshirt back and showed him the stitches in my wrist. I could see James' eyes flashing with alarm. I knew what I was doing. People saw what they wanted to see and believed what they wanted to believe. This would work. People were just too predictable.

"We're practicing for a play," I said, trying to keep my voice steady. I decided to ignore his other comment. School could wait. That dog thing could get up at any minute. I needed to make this quick. Brandon Cedar raised his eyebrows. James pushed back his hood. "It's just makeup."

"It's true, uh, dude." I cringed. *Don't lay it on too thick,* I thought at him. "You know, it's like a rendition of Tim Burton's *Corpse Bride* for the stage. Real cool, huh?" Brandon stared at the front door and then at the ruined patch of begonias and then he smiled.

"Mrs. Ruby," he said and stepped between James and me. There was an adult on the scene now, never mind the kids. Kids lie. Kids are trouble makers. I squeezed my fists in anger. James rested a hand on my arm.

"It'll be okay," he whispered as he followed the cop up to the house. *Please be normal,* I thought desperately. Grandma Willa was unpredictable. She could be talking philosophy one minute, staring at the wall in silence the next. I never knew what to expect.

"Brandon Cedar!" she exclaimed as he came to a stop on one of the front steps. "I never did thank you for bringing Tatum home after her and Maggie's little play sessions." I breathed a sigh of relief and grabbed James by the arm. I dragged him past the cop and Grandma Willa and into the pretty bedroom. I closed the door until there was just a little crack and leaned my ear against the opening.

James sat down on the bed and waited in silence. I could tell he was bursting to tell me something. *Should've thought of that last night when you were eating my Rice Krispies.* I stifled my anger. It wasn't really directed at him. I was coming down from an adrenaline rush. As soon as my body realized it wasn't a flight or fight situation, I'd be okay.

Mr. Cedar thanked my grandma with a promise to check up on us sometime next week and left. I sagged against the door with relief.

"I can't believe it," I breathed as Grandma Willa hummed her way up the stairs and disappeared into a bedroom.

"You should go thank your grandma before we go outside," he said, face serious. "She obviously cares about you." I scowled as I stood up and opened the door.

"She's just too senile to remember what happened," I said stomping over to the busted front door. *How'd we get away with that one?* James followed me quietly.

"She saw it, Neil," he said softly.

"She's crazy," I replied, avoiding his previous statement. "She has hour long conversations with my dead mother on a regular basis." I stepped out the front door and into the back of a harpy with a glowing bow clutched in her hand.

"It's lovely to see you again, Tatum," she breathed in a voice that was two parts Marilyn Monroe and one part harpsichord. I shied away from her and approached the dog thing. James stopped on the porch next to her.

"Thanks," he said, his macabre face lighting with a genuine smile. "I thought *Tatum*," he winked at me. "Was done there for a second." I rolled my eyes and never thought to wonder how the harpy knew my name when I'd never told her. That was the least weird thing I'd seen that night.

"The demon has been incapacitated," she replied simply, dropping her wings to the ground and gliding forward with long, graceful steps. Black feathers trailed behind her like the train of the world's most beautiful dress. My chest twinged with jealousy. I'd always wanted wings.

"Demon?" I asked, taking a step away from her. Despite the fact that she'd saved me from a pretty nasty attack, I still wasn't quite comfortable with the ethereally beautiful bird woman. Maybe I never would be. Her black lips twisted into a half smile.

"A soul that has been released but has not yet passed through or over. A wanderer, a lost one, a poltergeist." I held up a hand and she paused. I had the feeling that if I didn't stop her, she could go on forever. "You must pass him through," she said to me. I glanced back at James. He nodded. Action first, explanation later, I got it. I knelt down in the grass. Blood soaked into my jeans making me sick. *This isn't the same.* I told myself. *This isn't Boyd.* I squeezed my eyes shut.

Boyd is lying dead in a pool of dark.

You were minutes late.

It was your fault.

I opened my eyes with a gasp and jammed my fingers against the creature's warm skull. Its body disappeared as neatly and easily as the sandman's, but the blood remained. I struggled to get my feet under me and collapsed against the side of the house.

"Are you feeling well, Tatum?" asked the harpy lady. I closed my eyes and tried to swallow the clear night air into my aching chest. The blood on my knees was cooling rapidly. It was like having salt poured into a wound.

"I have to go," I said as I lurched towards the front door and into the house. I barely made it to the toilet before I was throwing up. My hair draped over my face and reminded me of my sister's dead body. I grabbed the edge of the sink for balance. *This is too much for me,* I thought as my fingers slipped off the granite countertop and I slumped against the wall. *I didn't want a new life. I didn't even want one at all.*

I put my head between my legs and tried to catch my breath.

I needed a break. Sleep. I needed sleep. I raised my face and stared at the red splotches on my knees. But first I was going to shower.

James was waiting in the hallway for me when I came out, but the harpy lady was nowhere to be seen. "Where's your friend?" I asked as I checked the tie on the white robe I'd found hanging in the bathroom. I think it had been Jessica's once. I didn't want to remember.

"She had to leave, but she did give us another assignment." James was smiling as if this were a good thing. I wished I could agree with him. I continued past him and through the foyer, past the sitting room, and through a set of pocket doors that led to the kitchen. I planned on going to sleep, but first I needed something to soothe my queasy stomach. Cereal was becoming my drug of choice. I almost felt like I couldn't get through the day without it. When I opened the blue box and found that nearly half of my remaining stash was gone, I almost flipped. But I had told James he could have it. I took a deep breath and went to the fridge. James sat down at the table and waited for me to join him.

"So, uh, I guess I should explain things a little better." I stared at him, the milk carton clutched tightly in my hand.

"You think?" I asked and tried to remember to check my temper. Taking my feelings out on him wasn't going to help, but I'd be damned if I didn't say it felt good. I took a deep breath and tried to force a smile. It felt awkward against my lips, like a mask that didn't fit. "I'm sorry," I said. James didn't ask what for, just nodded.

"You know," he began slowly, as if testing the waters. I stayed silent. "It was hard for me, too, at first." His voice trailed off in thought. I waited patiently, the sound of my spoon clinking against the china. "I couldn't stand the sound of cars for the first few months." He held one of his hands out in front of his face and studied the minute stitches that wrapped around his index finger like a spiral staircase.

"Because of your accident," I confirmed, wanting to break the quiet. A little quiet was okay, but too much left room for thoughts, memories. Pain.

"No," he said and his face fell. "Because of hers." I dropped my spoon, chipping the fine porcelain. *He's talking about his friend, Sydney. He feels guilty.* James stood up quickly and pushed his chair in. "I think I'll check in, if you don't mind?" He flicked some of his gray-brown hair away from his face. I wanted to beg him to stay, to tell me why there was a catch in his voice that told me he blamed himself. I nodded, my mouth stuffed full of cereal and curiosity. The questions could wait, they would have to wait. James was already walking away, his borrowed sneakers soft against the wooden floor.

I stayed at the table for awhile trying to satisfy my curiosity with food. It didn't work and I found myself in the living room staring at a painting Jessica had made. Ribbons dripped from purple clouds like rain and a girl under an umbrella hunched beneath an oak tree, her blonde hair tugged by an unseen tempest. I smiled and touched the canvas with my fingers.

Jessica had liked to paint with texture as much as color. The art was as vivid to my fingertips as it was to my eyes. "I miss you, Jess," I said as my heart contracted with longing. Death was supposed to have been my chance for a reunion, but now I was dead and I was still here, still suffering, still alone. "Why me?" I asked the girl in the painting. She didn't have an answer. Why should she? After all, the girl in the painting was me.

Movement outside the window caught my eye.

I weaved my way through the antique furnishings in the living room and into the adjacent sun room. The white harpy sat just outside on the sun bleached patio furniture. She was strumming a harp and humming a song I knew I'd never heard before. I opened the French doors and sat down on the edge of a chipped, cement bench. It had been nice once, but neglect and time had taken their tolls.

"Why are you doing this to me?" I asked her. She didn't look up until after she'd finished her song, tucking the harp beneath her right wing. Her face was sharp in the moonlight and her yellow lips shone like a beak. I wrapped my arms around myself to ward off a chill.

"I've done nothing to you, Tatum," she replied, folded her delicate hands in her lap. "Fate and circumstance chose you, not I." I bit my tongue to stop myself from saying something I'd regret.

"But why?" I asked. That seemed to be the million dollar question and nobody was willing to answer it.

"I cannot help you with that," she replied, tilting her chin up to meet the stars. "I can only assure you that I will do my utmost to guide your soul to peace." I wanted to tell her that she sounded like one of the new age books that Boyd had liked to read where everything was flowers and love and kindness. It was all bull, of course, but I'd let him tell me about how we'd be reborn in the next life and things would be good. "Karma's a bitch," he'd say. "But she's also fair, Neil. We've served our time. Next round's ours." I guess he really believed it.

"What was that thing?" I asked instead. I needed a distraction; I was starting to drown in pain again. I'd been treading water for way too long.

"Just think of it as a lost soul," she said simply, her voice tinkling like a wind chime. "And it's your job to guide it." She folded her wings beneath her and disappeared into the night leaving behind a sea of feathers and the harp.

I sat on the bench for awhile, watching the trees sway in the breeze and waited for clarity to dawn on me, for some lifelong revelation to hit me in the face like a truck. The void of emptiness inside of me yawned, stretching wide enough to swallow me whole. I squeezed my eyes shut and tried to breathe. Nothing happened. I wasn't ready for that first breath yet. It was still too soon. I opened my eyes and stood up.

The harp beckoned to me in the silence, begging to be strummed by expert fingers. I couldn't grant its request, but I did pick it up. It was lighter than I'd expected, like it was made from aluminum instead of wood. I traced my fingers across the grain and wondered how they'd gotten such a dark, almost silver stain. It reflected my face like a mirror, the moon silhouetted behind me like a spotlight. *The universe is watching you, Tatum.* I plucked one of the strings and closed my eyes.

The sound was pretty, but that was it. Nothing special had happened. I opened my eyes and frowned. Where was the magic? The mystery was there, that was for sure, but where was the hope that always accompanied a hero's journey into the unknown? I started to set the harp back on the bench when I noticed the inscription.

She lies twist'd, twist'd, twist'd,
On the edge of gray cliffs mist'd.

A shiver traveled down my spine as I moved into a brighter patch of moonlight to read. *Where have I heard this before?* I wondered as I finished the poem. It was only eight lines long, but the message was pretty clear. "This is about me." It was more of a statement than a question. "That fucking harpy has a lot of explaining to do," I snapped at nobody in particular.

I tucked the harp under my arm and stomped up to my room. I didn't worry about waking James or Grandma Willa. In reality, I almost hoped that one of them would wake up, join me in the hallway, and push away the loneliness that had crept back in like a fog. I needed a light like I needed air. I laid the harp on the windowsill next to the crows and wondered if I'd ever have one again.

CHAPTER ELEVEN

I adjusted the hem of the skirt I was wearing. It was too short for a funeral, but it was the only 'dress' that I had. I tried to ignore the stares of the old people in the aisles, their gray hair tucked under veiled hats or combed over to hide bald spots. Their glares made me feel like a fucking harlot for daring to show off my calves.

"You'd think I'd worn a red mini," I hissed at James as we sidled into a front bench next to the weeping widow. It sort of felt like *Harold and Maude* only James and I weren't here for fun, we were here for business. He gave me a ***tight-lipped*** smile but didn't respond. He was nervous and so was I. Today was our first real 'assignment.' James would touch the body or, as he'd corrected me earlier, at least somewhere in the vicinity so that the soul would be released from its earthly bonds. I would then step in and touch the ghost, sending it to the Akashic Library to study its past lives and hopefully, learn from its mistakes. I took a deep breath. It didn't seem so complicated anymore. It was actually a fairly simple concept. I just had to ignore the demons, the harp, and the creepy poem and it all made perfect sense. I sucked in another breath between my teeth. The widow looked up and glared at me.

I huddled down, burying myself in the gray wool coat that had belonged to my mother. Eight years later and it still smelt like ash. I shivered with unwanted memories. James wrapped his fingers around my hand. I stiffened. *You wanted a friend and now you've got the chance to make one. Do not blow this.* I pretended to yawn and pulled my hand away to cover my mouth. Boyd had been touchy-feely; James was touchy-feely. I guessed it was a good sign, but still, we'd only met four days ago. I wasn't sure if I was ready to hold hands yet.

James didn't look like he'd noticed. I sighed with relief. *Nobody will ever love you again,* my brain whispered sibilantly. *You had your chance. Boyd was a perfect match for you and you ruined it. You don't deserve friends.* I ignored my own thoughts. They'd gotten me nowhere. I tried to move my attention to something else. The sermon was just a bunch of crap I'd heard a thousand times before. *At Jason's funeral, at Dad's, at Mom's, at Abe's, at Jessica's.* Boyd hadn't gotten a real funeral, but then, I'd died for him, sort of. I supposed that was worth more than some empty words.

I surreptitiously flicked open the latch on my purse. The inscription on the harp whispered at me from inside the velvet folds. *Touch me, play me, sing me.* I snapped it closed. My newfound interest with the instrument was starting to border on obsession. I pushed that back, too.

James rose from his seat and I found myself the only person in the audience still sitting. I stumbled to my feet.

The widow approached the dais first. We waited in uncomfortable silence while the family said their goodbyes, dripped tears across the still face in the coffin, and had to be dragged away by friends. I stared at my feet intently. I didn't want to look at that, at other people feeling like I felt. It was too personal, too emotional. I blinked back tears.

James reached down and clasped my hand again. His skin was cold, at least physically, but somewhere deep down, something inside of me warmed. A bit of ice had been chipped away. I squeezed back and forgot to care that we barely knew each other. Loss is a powerful tool when it comes to getting to know someone.

James pulled me forward and I glanced up as we approached a man I knew only as 'Ray.'

His face looked peaceful enough and I could only wonder if he had died that way or if that congenial smile was the work of a skilled mortician. I was guessing it was the latter since James had told me that we were only sent to souls that needed help. "Most people can find the way to the library on their own," he'd told me on the walk over. He'd refused to drive and I understood that. Cars still weren't a comfortable subject for him. I didn't blame him. The idea of a trip to the beach sounded even worse than having to banish another demon. I bit my lip and tried to at least pretend that Ray's passing had been as peaceful as his face looked.

James raised his hand and brushed his fingers across Ray's wrinkled forehead. He was subtle about it. Even the widow with the hawk eyes latched onto our backs didn't seem disturbed by it. I could only hope I would do as well. I glanced around the room furtively.

"You might see an image, like a memory," James had said. "Like the one of … " He'd paused. He hadn't said Boyd's name which I appreciated. "Like before or you might not, like at the beach. It's hard to say. The dead are unpredictable. Their ghosts are formed by their thoughts and it's hard to say how people think. If you see nothing, touch the body, but make sure you only do it once."

I checked the room once more and saw nothing but unhappy faces and teary eyes. I pressed my fingers lightly in the same place that James had touched. Ray's skin was cool but not unpleasant to the touch. It was almost like he was one of the crows in my collection, frozen in time, unchanging as the world spun in a million directions. Nothing happened though I hadn't expected it to. A demon could only be summoned if I touched a memory from a person that was already at the library. I didn't know how I was supposed to tell the difference, but then again, that wasn't my job. That

114

was what the harpies were for.

James smiled reassuringly and pulled me down the aisle and away from the family. We'd invaded their pain for long enough. It was time to go.

"How do I know that it's done?" I asked James as we exited the church and paused on the edge of the stone steps.

"I can assure you that your current task was completed successfully." I turned around and found Ehferea standing in the shadows between the columns that lined the front of the building. "Your assignment is fifty percent complete. I will alert you to further action." I raised an eyebrow at her. A joke would've been appropriate, considering her stilted speech, but I wasn't in the mood for it yet. Time would tell if I ever would be again. "I have prepared your next assignment. Shall I brief you now?" I glanced over at James. He didn't look surprised, but then again, he'd been embroiled in this crap for over a year. He was probably used to it by now.

"That's it?" I asked him, ignoring the harpy. "We don't get a break? We banished a demon last night and passed through a soul today. That seems like a lot to me." James bit his lip but didn't answer. I pulled my hand away and surprised myself with the sense of loneliness that swept over my heart and covered it like a cloak. "This is not going to be my full time job," I snapped, overwhelmed with a sudden urge to go back to school. Normalcy called to me like a siren. *You can't have that ever again,* I told myself. *This is your life now. Death and pain are your masters.* I turned around and raced down the stairs without looking back.

"What do you think I should do?" I moaned at Boyd. He didn't respond, but that was okay. Just looking at him had helped cool my ire. It was hard to be angry when I was feeling so brokenhearted.

I had stopped at home to grab my backpack and found him in my room. It had nearly choked the life out of me. I had collapsed to the floor in front of my bedroom door and still hadn't gotten back up. Salt water pooled under my face and soaked into the untreated wood. We were playing cards. It was Gin Rummy, I think, but I was too worn out to care.

"You're telling me to ask my grandma about a woman that died over thirty years ago? She can barely remember *me* and I live with her." Boyd tugged at his beard and stared the ghost me down over the tops of the blue and red playing cards. "What?" I snapped at him as I threw the cards to the floor. From this perspective, I was aware that I had been throwing a temper tantrum. I had done that a lot with Boyd and he'd let me get away with it. I only hoped James would be as forgiving.

The door creaked open behind me. I rolled onto my back and stared in horror at Grandma Willa. Not once had she ever come up the stairs since I'd lived here. I'd been eight when I'd moved in and twelve when I'd moved to the attic. I was sixteen. It had been awhile to be sure.

"What's the matter, Tater Tot?" she asked, smiling warmly down at me. "There's no need to cry, Gram Gram's here." I hadn't called her Gram Gram since I was five. I rolled back over and ignored her. She would leave eventually. "You can tell Gram Gram anything," she said and I stiffened as her hands brushed my hair back from my face. She was kneeling behind me, her eyes focused on the ghost me sitting on the edge of my bed. "You're as pretty as your mother," she whispered, her face glinting with the sharp wit and acerbic tongue that she'd always tempered with homemade brownies and tomato slices with lemon pepper. I blinked at her.

"Grandma?" It was just one word, but in reality, it was a cry for help. I sat up and threw my arms around her, trying to be gentle at first but giving into the need for comfort. *Family.*

"Poor Tate," she whispered, her voice suddenly solid and without waver. "If the Rubys have ever had a fault, it's that we love too deep and too much. Your grandpa died of a broken heart when your mother passed away. They can call it a heart attack all they want, but we know better, don't we?" I sobbed into her shoulder. I didn't ask how she could see ghosts or demons or why there was always money in her purse when all I did was steal it, I just cried until there were no more tears left to cry.

"I'm sorry," I said to James as soon as I opened the door and found him standing there with his hands in his pockets and his face twisted with uncertainty and pain. This wasn't easy for him either, I knew that. I let him in and escorted him into the kitchen. Grandma Willa was knitting, lost in her own head again, but somehow, it was suddenly okay.

"Oh," she said, surprise wrinkling the edges of her mouth. "Marilyn, is this your new beau?" I ignored her and pulled out another chair to sit in. James smiled.

"It's nice to officially meet you," James said, holding out a hand. "I'm James and you must be Willa." Grandma Willa stared at his hand for a moment and shook it firmly.

"You can call me Willamina or Mrs. Ruby. My friends call me Willa and since you intend on dating my daughter, friend is the last thing I'm going to call you." She pulled her hand away and stood up, retreating to the parlor and her one hundredth read through of *Pride and Prejudice*.

"It looks like you two are getting along a little better," James said, avoiding the subject of demons and ghostly passings for the time being. "What happened while I was gone?" I ignored his question and drummed my fingers against the tabletop.

"Why did you run away?" I asked. He blinked at me, startled by the abrupt change in conversation.

"What do you mean?" he asked. I picked at a chip in the wooden tabletop.

"I know we're dead, but it's not like anyone would really notice if you covered these stupid things up." I rolled up the sleeve of the lace top I had worn to the funeral and flashed the stitches in my wrist. James sucked in a breath of air, puffed out his cheeks, and flopped into the chair Grandma Willa had been sitting in. I got that he had them on his face and neck and that I didn't, but why hadn't he tried to cut them off or cover them with makeup, Band-Aids, something? I wanted a friend more than ever. My brief moment with Grandma Willa had reminded me how important it was to have someone you could count on. Nobody else could understand me like James. He had that hurt and nagging guilt behind his eyes that I had behind mine and I wanted to know why.

"I know, right?" was all he said with a weak laugh that only belied how nervous he actually was. "Sometimes I think about what a coward I am. I see you doing things you don't want to do and sucking it up." I bit my lip and wished that were true. I had abandoned him earlier because I didn't want to be a summoner. Nothing could've been less true, but I decided to let him talk. He was this close to opening up to me. I could see it. He needed a friend as much I did. "You tried to go to school even though he wasn't there. You walk the same streets you must've walked together. You sit under the same roof. You look at the same stars." James paused as if collecting his thoughts. I stuffed my hands under my thighs to keep them from shaking.

"I couldn't do it, Neil. I couldn't stand to do the things Sydney and I had done together by myself. I couldn't even breathe the same air. It just hurt so fucking much." He bent over the table until his head was resting on his forearms. His muffled voice continued to pierce me inside where it hurt the most. "Some family is given to you, others you choose. I chose her. She was my family and it's my fault that she's dead." I opened my mouth to spill, to tell him everything, to reach down my throat and pull my heart out of my chest and spatter the walls with my fucking blood when the doorbell rang. I stood up, knocking my chair to the floor.

I could hear Grandma Willa sliding back the pocket doors that led to the front hall. I sat back down. She loved Jehovah's witnesses. I'd let her deal with whoever it was.

James and I sat in awkward silence. I reached up and touched the single purple earring in my right ear, trying to think of something to say. I'd lost the other at the beach. James sat still as death, his hands folded neatly in his lap and his gaze locked onto the tabletop.

Grandma Willa came into the kitchen with a big grin on her face. I could hear footsteps behind her, but she paused in the doorway, blocking whoever it was from view.

"Guess who's home, Tater Tot?" She'd traveled back in time again. I stood up from the table and ignored her, opening the fridge and grabbing the milk. Cereal was comforting and familiar. I would pour some for James, too, and then maybe he'd open back up and tell me what I so desperately wanted to hear. That I wasn't alone in the world. The Tupperware salesman or vacuum lady or whatever could leave. I wasn't in the mood to deal with that today.

"Neil." The strain in James' voice is what drew me back around.

I turned on my heel, prepared for the harpies, prepared for Jarrod or Margaret, prepared for the cops.

I dropped the carton of milk, watched the top pop off and drain liquid across the floor like white blood. A single word escaped the tightness in my throat.

"Jessica."

CHAPTER TWELVE

My dead twin was standing in my kitchen, a mirror image of me with bright blue eyes and blonde hair that shone like yellow copper. My first thought was demon, ghost, illusion. *She isn't anymore real than the Boyd that was in your bedroom this morning.*

"Tate." Her voice was pitched low, so soft she was hard to hear. She'd always been like that. I'd always been accused of being too loud and yet we had the same voice. It was just a reflection of how different we had become before she'd died. I looked to James for help. He replied to my unspoken question.

"I don't know," he said, hands held out like he was surrendering. I marched past Jessica and my grandmother, careful not to touch my sister. The Boyd-demon had been hard enough. I didn't need to have my sister breaking my collarbone or gnawing off the tips of my fingers. I shoved open the busted front door and looked around for Ehferea or Nethel. Neither was there.

"Tate." I spun around, backing up so that I was far enough away from her that there wasn't a snowball's chance in hell that we would touch. Memories bombarded my brain like a wave of bullets from a machine gun, each one finding their target. Boyd had been dead a week; Jessica had been dead two years. Neither was a very long time, but I had been able to block the pain of losing her with my friendship with him. Then, I'd kept that up by using the anguish of losing him to keep her memories at bay. Now, all of my walls were shattered and I was feeling anything and everything all at once. Suddenly, Abe's death was a fresh wound across my face. I could smell my mother's burning flesh. I saw images of my little brother, Jason, face down in our swimming pool. There was Dad on the news with the flashing words, *Bungee Jumping Accident Takes Father of Four.*

I threw up.

"Oh, God, Tate." Jessica tried to put her arms around me. I threw myself backwards. James stepped in front of me.

"Let's take it easy, okay?" he said, using the type of voice you might reserve for a frightened horse. *Just stay away from the hooves and you'll be okay.* I reached for my hood and realized I didn't have one on. I began to gasp for air. James knelt down and took my hands in his. He leaned his forehead against mine and started to whisper.

"Listen, listen here, Neil." I struggled against his grip. He started to babble, either for my comfort or his, I wasn't sure. "My mother was always kind of neurotic, you know? OCD. She cleaned the bathroom like three times a day and refused to let me do my own laundry. She always checked my shirts for blood. She'd heard somewhere that nosebleeds were an early sign of cancer." I swallowed a deep breath and nearly choked on it. James released my hands and pressed his against the sides of my face.

"Just breathe, breathe." I couldn't. It was like the breath I'd taken when I'd met Boyd, the one that had allowed me to live again, was being sucked right back out of me. "That's another reason why I didn't go home. It wasn't just about Sydney. My mother would've known. She was born in Athens, so I've always been kind of dark. The pale skin would've just freaked her out. It was better this way. Her son died in a car accident. Neat and clean. Like she always liked it."

I reached up and pulled his hands away from my face. I was starting to calm down again. Walls were being rebuilt, walls with James' pale face and stitched up lips. I swallowed a lungful of autumn air and nearly choked on it. It hurt going down, but once it started to pump through my veins, crisp as apples, I began to feel more like myself.

"I'm so sorry, Tate. I didn't mean to scare you." Jessica bent down next to me and laid a hand across one of mine. I screamed, startling her and James both. She stared down at me, confusion wrinkling a complexion I'd always been just a little bit jealous of. Aren't twins supposed to share the same everything?

She continued to watch me but didn't turn into a giant bat or a dragon or a fucking leprechaun. She just stood there and waited as patiently as I'd never been. I let James help me to my feet and tried to wrap my mind around what was happening. Jessica had been dead. I had seen her body. I had seen her blood. I watched her sleeping face in the coffin Grandma Willa had picked out, but I'd never liked. She'd been buried next to Grandpa and Mom and three thousand miles away from Abe and Jason and Dad. I couldn't articulate my feelings. My tongue swelled up and all I could say was, "What the fuck?"

Jessica smiled warmly and approached me softly, her arms held out in the question of a hug. I froze, stuck halfway between indecision and joy. *She was dead, but now she's not. She hated me before, but maybe she won't now?* I didn't move. Jessica's smile faltered.

"What's the matter, Tate?"

"Dead people don't come back to life." It was harsh and terse and I didn't really mean to say it, but I had learned my lesson. Boyd hadn't been alive at the trailer and by ignoring James' warning, I had turned him into a demon. I had wished for years that my mother would come traipsing through that door and whisk me away to our old house in Gresham. It hadn't happened and it never would. I walked right past her, into the house, and up the stairs. The progress I'd made with James and Grandma Willa seemed like nothing in the light of this, the worst cosmic joke ever played.

Jessica stopped me at the second floor. When I turned around, her eyes were swollen with tears. James was standing behind her, brow pinched with worry.

"Tattle?" I had hated that nickname when I was ten; I hated it now.

The sound of it broke my heart.

"Jessica?"

Jessica threw herself at me and knocked us both to the floor. She buried her face in my lap and told me she was sorry a thousand times over. James leaned against the railing and watched, trepidation tainting what was otherwise a happy smile. We stayed like that for a long time and all the while, as I brushed her hair back and she soaked my sweater with tears, I knew that something was wrong and I couldn't figure out what it was.

I hadn't stopped shaking since I'd seen Jessica, but I had started to think more clearly. She hadn't revealed how or why she was here or even acknowledged the fact that she was dead. That was fine for her, but I needed answers. I took the harp from my purse and left Jessica asleep in my bed. I hated to leave her there, but I didn't have much other choice. Both harpies were waiting for me when I walked outside.

"Explain," I said, holding the instrument out in both hands. I wanted to know about everything: the poem, the assignments, my dead sister. I'd been patient, but I couldn't wait anymore. "Tell me everything."

"We have another assignment for you," Ehferea breathed, her words more like the rustle of the breeze in the trees than someone's voice. I dropped the harp to my side in frustration.

"You already told me that," I snapped and, remembering James' words, added, "And I'll do it so can you please just answer some questions for me?" Ehferea's black lips pulled back from her tiny teeth.

"I have already briefed James on the previous assignment, but something else has come to our attention." Ehferea nodded and Nethel stepped forward, turning so that I could see the long, curving line of her back. Blood. Flesh. *Bone.*

I turned away.

"We have tracked a rogue spirit to this area." My heart flip-flopped in my chest and began to beat crookedly against my ribcage. *It isn't.* "We can't be certain of the form it has taken, but you can be assured that it has armed itself with a weapon from the Library." *It can't be.* "I suggest you use caution when approaching this spirit as it has the ability to turn others against you."

"Why are you telling me this?" I asked, my voice hollow and tinny, far away. Ehferea and Nethel exchanged stone faced glances. They were giving nothing away. I vowed not to, either. Three could play at that game.

"You and James have been assigned to dispatch the spirit to the appropriate realm. She has had an opportunity to study in the Library and has, regrettably, made the decision to use her time there in an inappropriate manner." Ehferea spread her wings and shook them, shedding loose feathers across the lawn, before tucking them more tightly against her body. *She's nervous.* I realized as she stared down her pointed nose at me. Her eyes were dark with specks of light, like stars. I realized with a start that she was actually quite pretty.

"So, all James has to do is touch her right?" I asked, keeping my voice steady. *I knew this was too good to be true. It has to be her. It has to be.* Ehferea shook her head, the mane of feathered hair that sprouted from her scalp shimmering in the late afternoon sun.

"You must use the harp to wrap her spirit. She will be sent to another plane for further assistance." I had always told Jessica to go to hell and now I was going to have to send her there. For what? For stealing some stupid weapon? *They haven't actually told you who it is.* My unconscious mind whispered soothing thoughts, but I knew. I'd known the moment I'd seen her something was wrong. I'd been right. I closed my eyes and fought down another panic attack. It's not like I had to do it. They couldn't make me. *But they could get someone else to do it. There must be other summoners around. Somebody sent Boyd to the Akashic Library and it wasn't you.*

I opened my eyes.

"What will happen to her there?" I asked, hoping I wasn't giving too much away. Nethel answered, her voice like a summer rain against the pavement.

"She was wronged in this life and finds herself unable to move forward. It does happen occasionally but rest assured, no harm will come to her." It wasn't really an answer, just a roundabout way of pretending they'd satisfied my question. I frowned.

"What am I supposed to do with this harp?" I lifted the instrument up again. "I've never been particularly gifted when it comes to music." Nethel smiled with her yellow lips and stepped closer to me. I watched her move slowly, fluid and graceful. If she wanted to hurt me, she could, no matter what I did. I stayed where I was and let her guide my fingers to the strings.

"It's quite simple, really," she whispered against my ear, pulling first my index and then my middle finger across a string. "It was made for you, after all."

I felt myself being swept up in music while a beautiful voice tolled the lines of the poem like an old church bell. *Wrong'd and ruin'd, broken down, our twist'd gatekeep, we have found.* I opened my mouth and sang a song I didn't know. Pretty words spilled from my lips and swelled in the air before coming to rest on my soul. The melody swirled around me as my fingers moved from string to string, strumming along with the words.

When the song was over, the harp tumbled from my hands and crashed to the grass, creating a divot and resting propped there, like the sword in the stone, just waiting to be picked back up.

I had crawled back upstairs and fallen asleep next to

my twin. When I woke up, she was gone and there was a note.

"Errands, Tattle. See you tonight for popcorn and a movie?

-Jessica."

The weirdness of the situation wasn't lost on me. I was aching for her, still shaking from the shock of seeing her again, and she, she was prancing around town in a sundress she was never supposed to wear again and kissing notes with lipstick that hadn't been touched since I'd found her with her wrists slit open and her head hanging in the toilet. She wasn't acting like someone that had just committed suicide. Then again, she'd been dead for two years. I guess she'd had time to get used to the idea.

I crumpled up the note and tried not to panic.

The harpies had assigned James and I to find her. What was the chance that they would also employ another summoner? I mean, she was *my* sister. There seemed to be some sick, fucked up thing with these people and watching me suffer. They'd want me to do it, wouldn't they? I realized I was pacing and paused when I heard footsteps outside my door. They were far too robust to be Grandma Willa.

"Are you dressed, Neil?" It was James. I rushed to the door and flipped the lock before he could reach the landing at the top of the stairs. Some part of me was ashamed, at my collection, at the book covers on the wall, at the pictures of Boyd strewn across the floor like a second area rug. Jessica had reinforced my insecurities with her looks of disapproval and the way she pinched her lips in displeasure. She'd done that before, but now that she was back and my heart was in her hand, it hurt more than ever. I couldn't handle anymore rejection. Besides, it smelt like decay in my room. I was going to have to find the crow in my backpack and get rid of it.

"Uh, no," I lied, bending down and retrieving a red hoodie from the floor. "But I'll be out in a minute." I threw on a pair of black jeans and Abe's old combats boots before drumming up some courage and unzipping my bag. I grimaced as I removed the plastic bag. The book with my brother's notes fell out of the front pocket and crashed to the floor with a fluttering of pages.

"Life is what you make of it."

I stared at the page for a long while before snapping it shut and tucking it into the purse where I'd stored the harp. It hadn't been much of a good luck charm so far, but I felt like nothing of Abe's could ever be bad. If there was even the slightest chance it might help me find Jessica before someone else did, I was taking it. I even took the pocketknife from my bedside table and stuffed it in the back of my jeans before heading downstairs.

James wrinkled his nose as I walked by and followed me to the outside garbage can.

"What's that smell?" he asked, waving a hand in front of his face. I ignored him and went back inside for the keys. When he saw what was in my hand, his face blanched. I squeezed my fist closed.

"You don't have to go with me," I said. "But I have to go find Jessica."

"What about our assignment?" James asked,

removing a sheet of paper from his pocket. An address was scribbled in barely legible handwriting. I paused. If Jessica really was this rogue spirit, maybe I could use our assignment to find her. As it stood, I hadn't even the slightest clue of where to start looking. I bit my lip.

"Okay," I said. Maybe I could kill two birds with one stone. The analogy came with another wave of the smell and I almost threw up again.

"The one question is," James asked, his face as wrinkled with displeasure as mine. "Do we have to drive?"

CHAPTER THIRTEEN

E xpecting to find a demon wasn't much different from not expecting to find one. It was scary as hell either way. I paused at the edge of the of the parking lot and watched a streak of white shimmer past the front gate and into one of the warehouses. I kept my eyes peeled for Jessica. James' head was down and if I wasn't mistaken, I didn't think he was breathing. Knowing we were technically dead and seeing proof of that were totally different things. I was starting to sweat, too, my fingers rubbing up and down the neck of the harp for comfort. James' anxiety was starting to wear off on me.

From the moment his hand had touched the door handle to the moment he stepped out on the gravel and used his foot to close the door behind him, James' face was even whiter than usual. The whole ride, he had gripped the edges of his seat with corpse stiff fingers and babbled. Whenever he got nervous, he started talking a lot. I had noticed it was one of his self defense mechanisms. Boyd had been the opposite. He had always gone quiet, like deathly silent. I'd been hard pressed to get an uh huh or a yeah out of him when he was like that.

"Are you gonna be okay?" I asked as we crunched across the wet ground towards the fading green of the warehouse. James gave me a thumbs up but didn't speak. I was actually sort of glad; he kind of looked like he needed to throw up. I felt bad, but it wasn't really possible to walk out to this part of town. It was a remote packing district on the north side, sandwiched between two major highways and tucked behind a meat packing plant. I tried to smile at him for reassurance and pretend I wasn't worried about getting thrown off the premises by the employees.

I adjusted the strap of my purse and hoped there wasn't going to be a confrontation. I didn't want the harp to fall out and break. Just the thought of something bad happening to it made me sick to my stomach. Despite the fact that I was even less sure of what was going on now than I had been before, I was almost grateful to the harpies. The instrument was starting to feel like a piece of my soul. It was strange and wonderful all at once. My brother, Abe, had always said that one song could change the world. I guess he was right.

James and I paused in the massive doorway, our eyes adjusting to the change from the bright, gray morning light to the pale flickering of the overhead florescent bulbs. It only took us a moment to spot it. I glanced over at James.

As soon as I saw his face, I knew something was wrong. He was watching the demon with wide eyes and quivering lips. It looked nothing like the other demons we'd seen, but then again, none of them had really looked alike.

"Are you okay?" I asked. He didn't respond. He didn't even look at me. Suddenly, he was falling and I was struggling with my arms under his. "James?" I asked, desperately trying to get a response. He was starting to freak me out.

"It's her," he said. It didn't take me long to figure out who he was talking about. Sydney. His dead friend. I recognized the pain in his eyes and the weakness in his limbs. That's how I'd felt when I'd seen Boyd. Lost. James was lost. I lowered him to the floor gently.

"Why?" he asked, his voice no more than a whisper. I didn't respond. I had no idea what I was supposed to say. *Because the universe is cruel. Because you told me yourself that if we don't see the one that started this then we won't know why we're still here.* I sat on the floor with him for a moment, holding his hand and wishing we were invisible. The demon hadn't noticed us yet, but if I'd learned anything by being around the others, it was that they were pissed. I glanced up and watched the white blur shimmer up and down the aisles like it was pacing. *Does she know who he is?*

Sydney paused and I was finally able to get a better look at her. She was actually quite pretty, for a demon.

Her fur was like virgin snow, untouched and perfect, and it fell from her lithe body in curling waves, like the branches of a willow tree. Her black eyes locked onto mine and for a moment, I thought I saw her there, deep down. There was a girl with strength and poise and inner beauty that never died. My heart jumped into my throat and I knew without a doubt why James had loved her.

"I tried," he whispered, grasping onto the edge of my sweater with cold hands. "I tried to keep her here. I've followed her and I've them at bay. Why now? Why?" I pushed him away and stared down at him in horror. Sydney didn't deserve to be a demon. I didn't know much about this new world I was now a part of, but I knew that. I had seen Boyd and the sandman and the red dog. They were angry and they didn't deserve to be. Death was supposed to be their time of rest. I shoved James from my lap and stood up.

Sydney was watching me carefully, her brown antlers lowered in anticipation of a fight. I wasn't going to give her the satisfaction. This was going to be quick and easy. The stitches in my belly itched and I vowed that I wouldn't be getting anymore. I approached her carefully, my eyes tracking her dancing hooves and her dark hair tangling in her antlers like kelp as she danced between stacks of boxes. All I had to do was touch her, once. I swallowed my fear and pushed forward.

She continued to prance, the long mane of her tail swishing back and forth like a cat's, until I had closed the gap between us and was standing within arm's length. Something inside of her must of recognized something inside of me because she lowered her head and paused, almost like she was surrendering to something bigger. I was shocked, to say the least. I had been expecting a fight, almost wanting one. Fights made more than just limbs ache. They took the mind away from the troubles that plagued it. A fight would've been welcome. My stitches twinged. Okay, almost welcome.

I reached my hand forward, not wanting to take any chances. She looked like a deer, maybe she was just acting like one, lowering her head for the charge. Fingers that were so pale they barely looked like they belonged to me anymore brushed against the feather white tips of her hair. I heard the scrape of sneakers on pavement and then I was falling.

My head slammed into the cement floor while roses of pain blossomed behind my eyes.

"Stop!" James screamed, the heavy weight of him draped across my weary shoulders like a shawl. "Don't, god, Neil, don't!"

"What the fuck are you doing?" I screeched. The pain was bad enough, but I could only imagine what it would feel like to have one of those hooves against my temple. I sat up too quickly and found myself collapsing against James' shoulder. He grasped me by my upper arms and locked his gaze to mine. There was desperation there, and fear. I recognized both because I felt them myself. *Is this what I'm going to be like when the time comes? Oh god, Boyd, I hope I can do it.*

He pulled me forward and tried to hold me against his chest. I wasn't ready for that kind of comfort, especially not after what he'd just done.

I looked around and tried to get a target on Sydney. She was gone.

"What the fuck were you thinking?" I snarled, throwing James' hand off of my shoulder. "You could've gotten me killed!" James shook his head.

"We can't die," he said, pointing at the dark X's across his throat. It was then that I realized that they were probably self inflicted. *Boyd's throat lies open like the Grand Canyon, wide and gaping.* I shook my head to clear it. Stars flickered in my vision and faded slowly, leaving splotches of blindness.

"Why?" My question was quiet but pointed. James pretended not to hear me and tried to stand up. I grabbed the hem of his sweatshirt. He looked away and didn't answer. I let him help me up because I had no other choice. Standing alone was not an option yet. I reached my hand up to my forehead and felt along the edge of my hairline. There wasn't a lump as I'd expected, but there was a small row of tight, neat, little stitches. I growled low in my throat. James startled as if I'd struck him. "Where is she?" I asked. James shook his head.

"I don't know," he said and then answered honestly with, "I've helped her escape, but I've never been able to communicate with her." I picked up my pace so that I wasn't next to him. If I had been, I might've punched him. *You have no right, you're just as selfish.* I ignored my nagging subconscious and stormed across the gravel, sending pebbles spraying across the parking lot like bullets.

"Please, don't be angry, Tatum." I froze where I

was standing and tried not to grit my teeth when I spoke.

"Don't you dare call me Tatum," I snapped, my anger at what he'd done seeping out through my pores. "My name is Neil." I continued walking. James caught up to me but didn't speak. I justified the pain in my head by matching it with the pain I saw in his eyes at the sight of the Seville.

We both climbed in and sat there in silence for several moments before I started the car. Light, autumn rain began to sprinkle across the roof in waves.

"I'm sorry," James said. He didn't elaborate and that was fine, we both knew what he was talking about.

"Don't be," I responded coldly. I was overreacting. I probably would've done the same, but still, when I thought of Sydney and that determination and that strength, I was mad. James was keeping her here for him, not her. I stepped on the pedal and drove it the floor. We peeled out of the parking lot and took to the highway like we were in a hurry. The fact that we hadn't seen hide nor hair of Jessica was starting to catch up with me. My dead sister had come back to life and I had no idea where she was or if she were safe. I had to find her.

"Where are you going?" James asked as I took an unfamiliar exit. The harp was singing to me from inside the purse and if I wasn't mistaken, if I wasn't just hearing what I wanted to hear, it was telling me to find her. I just had no idea where to look.

CHAPTER FOURTEEN

I drove the car to the mall, circled the parking lot but didn't get out. It didn't feel right. Jessica wasn't there. I tried downtown next.

"I'm so sorry, Neil," James said again. I continued to ignore him. I wasn't ready to talk. My head still hurt and the stitches in my forehead itched like hell. I didn't want to hear him speak.

"Leave me alone," I snapped, taking the wrong exit and realizing with anxiety that I was heading in the wrong direction. "I just want to find my sister." I squeezed the wheel with all of my strength and watched my knuckles pop through my skin, sharp and clear, like the backbone of the Boyd-demon. I shivered.

"I want what's best for her," James whispered, his

voice barely audible over the ever fattening raindrops and the whir of the motor. "I really do." I ignored him again. Jessica wasn't by the bookstore; she wasn't at the bakery or the bars. She wasn't downtown. I pulled back onto the highway.

"I released her, Neil," James continued, pretending as if there hadn't been a ten minute gap between his sentences. "I touched the road where I'd seen her die and I felt her spirit rise from the pavement like a curse. She wasn't happy, Neil. She didn't die happy." I didn't respond to that. I didn't want to. Pain crept up my spine like one of the demons we'd fought, saliva dripping from its angry mouth and burning like acid against my skin. Boyd hadn't died happy either. He'd killed himself and I still blamed me. I closed my eyes to regain my composure and almost crashed. James said nothing, but I could see that the longer we were in the car, the more it was affecting him.

I stayed out longer on purpose.

After Old Town, after the Plaza, after the Fourth Street Market, I had searched just about everywhere I could think of except the beach, but even for Jessica, I wasn't willing to go back there yet. I sighed and gave up, turning the car back towards home. I was going to have to trust that she'd come back. It was a hard thing to accept, but I'd been given no other choice.

When I pulled into the driveway, I got out first, leaving James in the passenger seat, and ran inside, searching each and every room and calling my sister's name. She wasn't there and it was starting to get dark. I took a deep breath and approached Grandma Willa. She was hunched in her favorite rocking chair and halfway through a blue and purple sock. She paused in her knitting to look up at me.

"Hello there, Tater Tot, are you hungry?" I frowned and tried to reconnect with the hug that she'd given, the desperate search for human connection that I'd found in her arms.

"Have you seen Jessie?" I asked, purposely using my sister's childhood nickname. Grandma Willa shook her head and I felt my heart catch in my throat. Jessica still wasn't back yet. I checked the cuckoo clock on the wall above the couch. It was only three o'clock. It still wasn't too late for her to come home. I went back outside and checked for the harpies. They were gone and so was James. A momentary stab of panic entered my chest. *What if he's left, too?*

I ran back inside and checked the pretty room. James was sprawled across the bed on his stomach. His head was buried in one of the pink pillows and his sweatshirt was draped over him like a blanket. I decided to leave him alone. He needed time to process; I needed time to understand. I ventured back up to my room and stood with uncertainty in the doorway. It was the first time in days that I'd had the freedom to do anything. There were no responsibilities, no assignments, no dead people. I breathed in the air that still smelt a little bit like decay and sat down on the edge of my bed, fingers twitching with anticipation.

I didn't know what to do. Reading seemed like a far away treat, a worm dangling in the distance from a fisherman's hook. If I took the bait, I might never come back. I avoided my book collection and glanced at my laptop. All I'd ever done on that was study taxidermy and order supplies or talk to Boyd, one of which was no longer appealing, the other, no longer possible. I tucked the sweatshirt into my mouth and sucked on it. The antique clock ticked by in warning. *You only have so much time left,* it said. *Make the most of it.* I stood back up and paced.

Hours later, I found myself on my bed, belly down, rereading the book I had finished the day Boyd died. My brother's notes were still as engaging, still as beautiful, as the day I'd dismissed them as nothing. I still didn't believe what he'd written. Maybe I believed it even less now. Still, it didn't matter. What mattered was finding Jessica and embracing her and Grandma Willa. They were the family I had left. I had to make them count.

I rolled onto my back and closed my eyes, pulling the book and a picture of Boyd tight against my chest.

Why can't I go back in time and be a normal kid in a normal place with a father that doesn't die the day before her third birthday, and a mother that still cares, and a little brother that's watched and doesn't drown? Why can't I go back and tell Abe not to go to that concert? Why, oh why, can't I save Jessica and Boyd?

I threw the book to the floor and tried to remember that James, despite our short time together, was the one that was teaching me how to breathe again.

"Why are you doing this to me?" Boyd says. I look away because I can't take the pain in his eyes, the feelings of hurt and betrayal. I did that. Me. He's sitting in his bed with the covers crumpled around his waist and I think he might be crying. I pretend not to notice and bend down to tie my sneakers.

"Are we going to that concert on Friday?" I ask. Avoidance. I have always relied on avoidance to help me get through things. This was my own fault, but it makes no difference. I pretend not to hear his next question.

"Do you love me?" he asks. I sit up and huff, adjusting my hood angrily. He knows that I love him but not in that way.

"What am I supposed to say to that?" I snap, turning and facing the mirror that backs Boyd's bedroom door. James' face stares back at me. It's a symbol of how similar we are. I just don't know to what extent yet.

"Don't leave like this." Four words that mean nothing and everything all at once. I leave and I know in my heart that a few, short months later, this is what kills him.

When I woke up, blonde hair was plastered across my lips, suffocating me. *I'm drowning in memories and pain.* I reached up and peeled it away from my face, taking a hot, heavy breath of the stagnant, attic air. I pushed my aching body up, my back screaming at me in protest from sleeping twisted, and propped open the single window. The night was alive with sounds and movement, both foreign and familiar. I suddenly wished I could speak its language, but then, I've never really been the outdoor type. I checked the attic clock, tilting it so that the moonlight illuminated the numbers enough for me to read. It was late. Ten o'clock and still no Jessica. I changed into a fresh set of clothes, another pair of dark jeans, a purple hoodie, and a pair of yellow Converse that Boyd had gotten me for my birthday. He'd felt guilty since they were from the thrift store and not new. I didn't care. I had hugged him and told him that they were perfect. I wished I'd told him how perfect he was as a friend.

Guilt nibbled at me as I walked down the stairs slowly, trying not to wake either Grandma Willa or James. I felt like I'd been dipped in a pool of piranhas. Each little memory, each mistake, each wrong word was like a piece being bitten off of my soul. I should've been nicer to Boyd. *I should be nicer to James.*

I checked the upstairs bedrooms for Jessica and then went down the second set of stairs and stood by the door to the pretty bedroom. The lights were off. I tried the door handle gently. It was unlocked.

James was lying exactly as I'd left him, on his belly with his arms folded under his face. It was hard to tell in the dark, but I was pretty sure he was sleeping. I paused in the doorway for several minutes and tried to justify my behavior towards him earlier. He loved Sydney and he wanted her to be with him. I got that, but I had to find her and send her to the Library. As soon as I found Jessica, I would go. It might hurt at first, but he would thank me for it later when we sent her on. He could say goodbye for real then. I squeezed my eyes closed and blinked back tears. I had to do this and hope that, when the time came, he would do the same for me.

"I'm sorry for how I treated you earlier," I whispered, wishing that I could have this kind of frank discussion with a person who was actually awake. Avoidance. There it was again. I took a deep breath and opened my eyes. "I only did that because I ... I see myself in you, James. Thanks for trying to make friends with me. It takes a brave guy to do that." James shifted and for one, terrible moment, I thought he was awake and that he'd heard me, but he just adjusted himself and fell still again. I turned on my heel and left.

I searched the rest of the downstairs bedrooms for Jessica and decided with a small spurt of anxiety that she definitely wasn't home and hadn't been back since she'd initially left that morning. I opened the front door and walked to the end of the yard, pausing under the shadows of one of the old trees. Anita had told me what kind they were before, but I'd forgotten. Standing beneath them made me want to know. They were majestic and old and strong. I envied them their peaceful lives.

I sighed with frustration and glanced up and down the now quiet street. It wasn't like I expected to see her there, but I needed to do something. Now that my body was rested, the idea of sitting down just seemed ludicrous. Time was short. People were short lived. I needed to find my sister and I needed to do it soon. I was turning around to go back inside when I saw the school out of the corner of my eye. I hadn't thought to look there yet which was actually pretty stupid. Jessica's life had been school. Sometimes, I had thought she cared more about what the people at school thought about her than what I did.

I ran upstairs, retrieved the harp, Abe's book, and the pocketknife. I thought about waking James, but I knew if I did, I'd have to tell him what Nethel and Ehferea had said. I'd have to admit that I was the world's biggest hypocrite. I decided against it and took off into the night, hoping my meager weapons would be enough to fight off any attacks against my heart. I couldn't lose her yet. We needed more time together and if she did have to go, if it was really what was best for her, then nobody could do it but me. I walked faster.

The night transformed the school into an asylum in my mind. The bars over the first floor windows were there to keep patients in and not students out, the gate was locked tight to hold back hordes of the insane and not to prevent graffiti artists from practicing their craft. Everything evolved into something else until it came to the point were I was pacing the front wall instead of climbing over it. I looked down at the ground beneath me and debated leaving. I could go back to the house, wake James up and tell him everything. Then, tomorrow we would come back together and look for Jessica. Maybe she would even come home?

I sat down on the bricks and let my feet dangle over

the edge towards danger. I'd never been a coward. I'd been a lot of other horrible things for sure, but I'd never been that. I took a breath, like I was preparing to dive, and leapt down.

There were security cameras all over the front of school but none along the sides where the forest still ran a bit wild and used condoms littered the floor like leaves. I rolled my eyes at my peers and at the adults who thought they could control them but never really did.

I didn't find Jessica in the forest, or behind the gym, or in the quad where the basketball players hung out and practiced at lunch. The saddest part was, I wasn't even really sure where to look for her. We had gone to school together here and yet, I had no idea where she'd liked to hang out. I was about to give up when I crossed by the path that led down a hill, through some trees, and to the football field. Jessica hadn't played any sports, but she had always gone to the games. It made sense that she'd be there.

I flipped off the security camera that was blinking its red eye at me from the edge of the art building and started down the pathway. The evening's rain had made the steps slick and difficult to navigate. It was a slow process going down, my heart racing faster by the second. It was like the climax in a good book; the anticipation was killing me.

When I finally reached the field and found nobody there but a flock of crows, I screamed in frustration. The birds took to the air in a series of squawks and feathers and then there was nothing but the moon and me. I cut across the grass towards the ag building and the place where I'd first discovered that Jessica wasn't a virgin anymore. I frowned at the memory.

I could check there. It wasn't like I could go inside, but there were some animal pens and a shed. They were probably locked tight, but it couldn't hurt to try. I chastised myself for missing out on the obvious. Every time I thought I had checked everywhere, there was somewhere else. *I'm never going to fucking find her. You didn't know her well enough so now you're screwed. You have no idea where she is or why she's there.*

I did a half-assed search of the area and came up empty again.

I took a longer but less slippery route back up the hill and was in the process of climbing over a different section of the wall when I heard voices. Well, they more like moans really, but I had to check. I wouldn't forgive myself if another grim reaper or summoner or whoever found her while she was fucking because I was too much of a prude to check.

Sure enough, it was her.

My breath caught painfully in my throat and I almost vomited again.

Jessica was wearing my clothes.

She had on my green, "Kiss Me and You're Dead; I'm Not Fucking Irish!" sweater and the black skirt I'd worn to the funeral. Abe's boots were pressed into the mud, spread apart to allow whoever it was to fuck her. I gnawed at my lip and forced myself not to look away. It wasn't easy; the image was burning me in more ways than one. I tucked my hands into the sleeves of my sweatshirt and put them to my mouth to stop myself from screaming. I wanted to stop her, to take her home and tell her she was worth more than that, but I didn't know how to do it. I was going to have to wait.

When they were finished, Jessica stood up and brushed herself off, twisting the skirt so that it was back in place and pulling leaves from her hair. When she moved forward, the moonlight caught her face and highlighted the purple earring in her ear. Boyd's earring. My earring. I almost jumped down and tore it from her flesh. Even dying hadn't stopped our sibling rivalry. I glared at the black kohl around her eyes and tried to understand why she would dress like me, pose like me, *fuck* as me.

And I'd been worried about her.

"Nice to know you're not as cold as you look," the boy said, zipping up his pants and caressing her arm in a way that made my stomach twist with nausea. It was Jarrod Rhodes, Margaret Cedar's current boyfriend, and Jessica's ex. I hadn't thought she cared about any of the boys she'd fucked, but yet, here she was, with a second chance at life and she was spending it in the forest with a boy that thought it was funny to tease people about their dead friends.

I waited in silence. I suddenly didn't want to talk to her anymore. I suddenly wished she were still dead.

Why did you do this? I thought at her. *Why did you come back and torture me like this? I missed you so much; I loved you so much. You were the last person I had left and you abandoned me in more ways than one.*

I felt my heart breaking in two.

"Come with me, I want to show you something," she said, taking his hand in hers. I almost left, almost went and tried to find Sydney, but my feelings for her ultimately topped my anger. She was my sister and I had to be here for her. I followed them back down to the football field.

"You know, Tate," Jarrod said to Jessica as I watched and fumed behind the bleachers. "You were better than your sister was." I froze, but all Jessica did was giggle and flick her hair over her shoulder in a way I would never would. I guess he thought it was a compliment. It made me sick.

"You're so silly, Jarrod," she said, reaching into the purse she had picked up from the forest floor and slung over her shoulder. It was white and cream with brown buckles and it definitely wasn't mine. "That's why I wanted to meet you here. I wanted to give you a second chance." Jarrod scratched his head and glanced over his shoulder like he was looking for a way out. The fun was over, time to go home. Jessica reached up and turned his face towards hers. The glint in her eyes was hard as flint and it gave me the chills. "There is good in you, Jarrod," she said through her teeth. "I can see it, but you have to let it out. I love you, Jarrod. You have to accept that you are I meant to be together." I blinked in shock at the same time Jarrod took a startled step backwards. It was like watching a scene from *Fatal Attraction* only instead of Glenn Close, the stalker woman was played by my twin sister.

"What the hell?" Jarrod mumbled as he backed up another step. Jessica was opening her purse slowly, the glint of metal inside raising the hairs on my arms. She was going to shoot him?

Apparently, Jarrod thought so, too, because he

turned around and started to run. I moved out from behind the bleachers.

"Jessica!" I shouted. If she shot him, it was all over. For her, for me, for everybody because I would be immortal and I would be rotting in jail and somebody else would come for her and Boyd, and James would go on protecting Sydney in a way he shouldn't have. She looked up at me, but she didn't seem surprised. She was smiling. She pulled her hand from the purse. In it, was a flute.

The harp pulsed at my hip, making me gasp.

The weapon the harpies had mentioned. It wasn't a sword or an axe or a bow; it was another instrument. That scared the shit out of me. If my harp could wrap souls and transport them to another dimension, if it could make music with just one touch and open my throat and make me sing words I didn't know, what could hers do? Jessica put the metal to her lips.

Jarrod was still running, he hadn't seen the flute, but when he heard the music, low and sweet, he paused and turned back around. His pasty face was red and his eyes rimmed with worry. I watched as that worry transformed back into arrogance. He hadn't seen me yet, just a girl with a flute who had told him she loved him.

"I don't want to be with you, you fucking psycho," he growled, using his fear as fuel for his insults. "You death obsessed creep. You were a fuck and nothing more, a nice piece of ass." Jessica closed her eyes and I felt myself getting angry as I watched pain flash across her face. Did she kill herself because of him? I glared down at Jarrod and hoped not or next time, it might be me with a gun in my purse.

I opened my mouth to say something, to draw his attention to me and let him see that a ghost had crawled from the grave. *Try telling insults to a dead girl.* A whirring noise stopped me from saying anything.

A demon passed over the field in a blur of metallic and crystal. When it came back around, I saw that it was long and thin with eyes like a dragonfly and legs like a spider. Its gossamer wings cast prisms across the grass and turned it into a kaleidoscope.

Jarrod screamed.

Jessica pulled the flute away from her lips and gave Jarrod an ultimatum that chilled even my blood.

"I'm warning you, Mr. Rhodes," she said, stalking forward like a suicidal ghost and most definitely not like a fifteen year old, should've been sixteen year old, girl. "This is your last chance. You either choose to be with me or I will *make* you be with me. You have no other choice. I love you. I love you more than air, more than water, more than *life*." Her voice cracked on the last syllable and brought tears to my eyes. She was crazy, but she was also in love. It was ugly but beautiful. I watched the demon circle and found myself unable to move. I didn't know what I was supposed to do. *You could send her on*, I thought, but one look at Jessica's face and I knew I wasn't ready yet. We needed to talk first. I needed to know that she loved me and know that she believed, without a doubt, that I loved her.

Jarrod wasn't listening. He wasn't even looking at her. He was crouching on the ground and shrieking in terror at the unfamiliar.

I almost joined in when I felt a hand on my arm. I whirled around and came nose to nose with James. He was breathing hard and nibbling the stitches in his lower lip.

"I followed you but don't be mad," James blurted in a rush. "I was awake and I heard you leave. I heard your apology and I'm sorry, too." He paused and took a deep breath, his eyes boring into my soul like nobody else's ever had. I took a nervous step back. "Let's help each other," he whispered and turned his attention back to the field.

I followed his gaze and saw that Jessica was now leaning over Jarrod and whispering. A knife glinted in her hand, reflecting the moonlight and the single purple earring. I turned to James with a question in my eyes.

I love her and I don't know what to do.

James took my hand and pulled me down the stone steps and onto the field.

The dragonfly demon circled above us, diving occasionally as if it were testing the waters, but it never came within striking distance. Jessica was controlling it as Ehferea had said. The powers of the flute stunned me and I ended up stumbling. James pulled me to my feet and kept going.

"She can't kill him," was all he said as he dragged me and my indecision along for the ride.

Jessica rose from her crouch and stepped back, replacing the knife in her purse. When she turned to face us, she was smiling again, but it was tinged with sadness and regret and slashed with a bright red splatter of pain. She was hurting and it was twisting her in ways that it hadn't twisted me. It was scary.

James and I paused, not wanting to get too close but unable to move away. Jarrod was a piece of shit, but she couldn't kill him. Things wouldn't be right that way. It wouldn't make her right; it wouldn't take away the pain he'd caused her. It could and would only make things worse.

"Jessica?" I ventured. She glanced away from me.

"I loved him, Tate," she said and her voice was soft. It gave me hope. Hope that, when she turned back around, was drowned by the look of desperation in her blue eyes. She would do anything for Jarrod, or to at least she'd do anything to have him. She probably couldn't tell the difference anymore. "I still love him. He's my soul mate and I can't go on without him." She blinked back tears as James squeezed my hand for comfort. He tangled his fingers in mine and told me without words that he was there now. We were friends. Pain would bind us together tighter than any cord; death had made us equals, the harpies had made us partners, but pain, pain would make us friends forever.

"I tried to study, Tate. I looked at the books and I saw myself for what I was. Useless. I saw Daddy and Jason and Mom and Abe and I … " She paused and her voice trailed off, drowned by the whirring of the dragonfly's wings. When she spoke again, her tone was firm and strong, like she was declaring a hard truth but a necessary one. "And I saw you. You were the only person that was ever there for me. You were the only person that loved me as me." Tears burned my eyes and I tried to go to her. James held me back. I had to trust that he was right and stayed where I was. He wasn't thinking clearly with Sydney and I wasn't thinking clearly with Jessica. We needed each other's guidance.

"I knew that when I found the flute, it was destiny. I could control spirits, demons, ghosts, souls. But you," she paused again and glanced back at Jarrod. He was lying on the grass in a fetal position. I didn't see blood, but he wasn't moving. I exchanged a look with James. "You didn't know I was there. I watched you move on without me, meet Boyd, love Boyd, and I wanted you, but I couldn't take you away from that." She shook her head and tears glittered for a brief moment in the air, like crystals, bits of pain that glimmered like stars. "It was like watching me and Jarrod." I was shaking my head now, too. I loved Jessica, but I loved Boyd just as much. She couldn't compare this to that. I would have never done these things to him.

"I stayed with you and watched, fed off of your love. It was what kept me alive and safe, but then when Boyd," she cut off again and stared me down, hands shaking. She had loved him, too. I could see it. She had shared moments with us that nobody else knew about. She had been a part of it all and she missed him, too. I buried my face in my hands and sobbed. James pulled me to his chest and let me cry. I barely knew anything about him, but it felt good. He understood me, us, this. When Jessica spoke again, her voice was so quiet I could barely hear, but her words were loud enough that they pierced me to the soul.

"When Boyd died, I saw you were in pain. I just wanted to comfort you, to hold you again, and the only way I knew how to do that was to bring you over.

Running scared, alone and tortur'd, Twist'd by demons, blood, misfortune. I had to do it. It was written on the flute, Tate. It was about me; it was made *for* me," she whispered fervently as my heart broke into pieces and refused to be put back together. "I had to follow my destiny, Tate. I had to kill you."

CHAPTER FIFTEEN

S *ticks and stones may break my bones, but words will never hurt me.*
I swallowed my heart and buried myself in James' sweatshirt. It was intimate, it was comforting, it should've made me happy, but her words refused to leave my head.

"I had to kill you."

Sticks and stones may break my bones, but words will never hurt me.

The mantra didn't help. The stones had hurt; they had killed me when she'd pushed me from the cliff, but the words hurt, too. She didn't love me more than she loved herself. I knew that because I knew I loved her more and I knew I would've never done something like that. I sobbed and soaked James with my tears and my misery and my suffering.

"I tried to kill a harpy, Tate. I tried for two years. One taste of a harpy's flesh and I could've been whole; I wouldn't have had to kill you. You could've seen me then!" I refused to look at her. She wasn't processing any real emotions and her voice was hollow and imperfect and disgusting to me. I didn't know how I would feel if I looked at her. "But it never happened and then you were so sad." She took a shaking breath. James squeezed me more tightly and laid his chin on my head.

They say that disasters bring people closer together, that people that go through hurricanes or floods or bombings, that they form bonds that make them seem as if they've known each other for years. That was happening to James and I in that moment. Four days was becoming four years. *I will appreciate this later,* I promised myself as my sister dug herself further and further into the hole of my heart.

"But I've done it now," she said, almost jubilantly. She was excited, excited about eating a piece of flesh, of beautiful Nethel's back. She hadn't shown me pain, but what I'd seen was horrible; it had to hurt. "Jarrod can see me now and I can have him, too, and I'm sorry, Tate." I could hear her taking steps towards us. James slid the pocketknife from the back pocket of my pants. I heard him flick it open. When Jessica spoke again, her words were testy and uncomfortable. "I never thought you'd get called by one of those devils. I thought you'd be a spirit and I'd play my flute and you'd come to me and we'd get Jarrod and we'd walk together and ... " She paused in her rambling and I spun around to face her.

"I loved you more than anything and you left me," I said and I realized I was still crying. "You left me alone and then you took something that wasn't yours, Jessica. You took my life when I never really had one. Now, look at me!" I gestured at the stitches in my wrist. "I'm not me anymore, I'm something else and now I have to say goodbye to Boyd for the second time and I ... " I brushed my fingers against the purse. It was time to let her go. I wasn't going to get the talk that I wanted. I wasn't going to be able to hold her and have a memory to light the dark nights and chase away the fog. She had lost it. She had lost it and she had lost me. I would still love her, I always would, but that didn't mean I had to like her.

Movement to my right caught my eye.

Jarrod was sprinting across the field, his shoes kicking up divots as he stumbled and tried desperately to get away from something that never should've been. Jessica frowned and the dragonfly demon reacted. I don't how it knew, but somehow, it was responding to her wishes. It dove at Jarrod's head, its spindly legs outstretched, clawed tips coruscating with moonlight.

"Stop it!" I screamed, unable to stop the demon but throwing myself at Jessica. I didn't know if it would help, but it was all I could do. I could hear James moving behind me. I think he was headed towards the demon. I didn't get a chance to look because Jessica turned too quickly and I found myself on the ground. She flipped me over and straddled me while I struggled to get a hold of her hands. She had the knife. My sister, my twin sister, had a knife and I had no idea if she would use it on me.

She was crying again, her eyeliner dripping down her face in wet clumps. Her hair was a mess, like a golden halo, fanning behind her head and blocking my view of the sky.

"You know," she said, gulping down more sadness and pain with each breath. "It was hard enough to kill you the first time; think about how I feel. I have to kill my own sister, *twice*." She sat up, satisfied that with the wet earth that I was sinking into and the force of gravity, that she had the upper hand.

"Why?" I asked her, finding no comfort in the fact that I couldn't die. The idea that she was even going to try to kill me, that I'd have a permanent reminder etched into my skin in black thread, was enough to smash my soul into bits. I gazed up at her, my arms straining against her shoulders as her eyes lost more and more of her focus and her sanity and wished that I were nothing but atoms. That I was just molecules and elements and space, that I had no soul and no feelings and no heart. It hurt; it all hurt so much.

"Don't be sad, Neil," Boyd had said. "Because when you're sad, it feels like there's nothing right in this world."

I watched her watch me and squeeze the hilt of the knife and I let everything I ever wanted to say drip from my eyes and soak into the neck of my sweater, but she wasn't listening. I hiccuped and wished that the knife would kill me and then the harpies could send a summoner and I could go to the Library and stop being a part of this world that had wronged me and beaten me down at every opportunity.

Jessica smiled a horrible smile that mocked my pain and twisted my soul.

"Did you know," she began, leaning down and with a start I realized that there was excitement in her voice. She wanted to kill me. She wanted me, not as me, but as something that would validate her own sense of self. "The only way to kill a summoner is with a knife, soaked in the blood of a loved one?" My eyes widened in shock. Summoners could be killed? *But we're immortal,* my brain screamed, suddenly afraid of the one thing it had always wanted most. Death.

My body overrode my soul and fought. It fought like a caged animal that knows that when the gates open, the hunter will be standing there waiting, rifle in hand. I screamed with a fear I hadn't known I had. *I don't think I'm ready to die yet,* I realized as I opened my throat and spilled my terror into the night air. *I haven't even had a chance to live.*

Jessica slid the knife across her wrists in a cruel imitation of how she'd ended her own life. Blood boiled from her skin and fell in fat drops, scalding me, burning me. I struggled harder, but I couldn't get her to move. She sat atop my ribcage and squeezed her thighs, locking me in place. I didn't know if it was supernatural strength or just belief in her own, confused conviction. *She's stronger than you. You can't escape this.* I closed my eyes as she lifted the knife. I didn't want to see it. *Just make it quick,* I thought as tears pushed their way past my eyelids. *Just do it and play your flute and wrap me under your spell so I don't have time to think about how you betrayed me.*

Thunder rumbled in the distance and suddenly, there was a lightness on my chest. I could breathe. I opened my eyes and saw Jessica and James struggling in the grass. I sat up quickly and wiped the blood from my face. Jarrod was gone and so was the demon. It took a moment for me to get moving. My emotions were running wild, thoughts I'd never had were fighting for attention, and a sense of relief was washing over me, nearly drowning in its intensity. Finally, I forced my shaking legs to stand and joined in the fight.

James and Jessica were grappling over the knife. His hand was clamped around her wrist while she tried to force her way into his flesh. She was winning.

I put my hand around hers and tried to peel her fingers away from the blade. When she looked up at me, I almost faltered. There was betrayal there, too, and hurt.

"You're choosing him over me!" she screamed as the knife flew from her fingers and toppled end over end across the damp grass. James released her and stood up, brushing dirt from his pants. In his hand he held her purse, snatched right from her shoulder in the tussle. She'd made the mistake of paying attention only to the knife and had lost her most precious weapon. Without the flute, she wouldn't be able to stop me. I was going to send her on and I was going to do it now.

"I love you, Jessica," I said as I reached for my purse. "No matter what you've done to me." I heard James gasp and turned to find him holding an empty bag. Sweet music poured from Jessica's lips and spread out across the field and into the trees. A crash resounded, scattering birds and shaking pine needles to the earth. Something big was coming. I exchanged a look with James. He didn't know about the harp, but if he'd had, I was sure that he'd want me to use it. I flicked open the clasp and reached for it.

No sooner had my hands brushed the silver wood than it was gone. My purse was flying across the field like a football and I was face down, an intense pressure on my back and neck. I could hear James screaming in the background as I was lifted up and slammed against the base of the goal post. Tentacles twisted around my belly and squeezed until I was blue in the face. My brain told me I was dying, but I didn't black out. I couldn't. I was *indefinite.*

"Why, Tate?" Jessica asked as she stepped over James' body. He was lying unconscious at the fifteen yard line, blood seeping from the back of his neck. A blue demon circled him with hair like glass and the face of a baboon. I wanted to shriek at James to get up, but I couldn't find the strength for breath. *He'll be okay; he can't die. He's indefinite, too.* "Why do you always do this to me?!" she screeched, doubling over and stumbling like it was too much for her to bear, like I had wronged her and the weight of it was driving her to her knees.

I tugged at the black tentacles around my waist, but they were solid muscle. I couldn't even get my fingers under them for leverage. The demon behind me shifted and I could feel hot breath against my neck. I refused to look.

"Why do you have to go out of your way to make things difficult?" she asked, tapping the flute against the palm of her hand. With my sweatshirt and Boyd's earring and Abe's boots, it was like watching me punish myself. I had always done it, in some form or another. I had punished myself for the deaths of those around me. Now, I was finally starting to get outsider's view on how ridiculous I had been. *I'm going to have a revelation and then die. How Shakespearean.* "You wanted things to be hard for me. You couldn't just blend in; you had to stand out in the worst way, Tate. What is wrong with you?" I blocked her voice out and went to that place inside my head, the place I'd gone when I'd found Boyd dead.

Just as I found myself in a meadow with gently swaying daisies and a blanket with the world's best picnic, an arrow shattered my concentration and drew me back. It struck the baboon demon in the chest, knocking him away from James just as Nethel landed in the grass, light as the feathers that coated her skin and wings. Ehferea fired a second arrow and I watched in horror as it came straight at my face – and then past it.

The arrow struck the thing behind me and I found myself falling.

I landed on the ground with a grunt and sucked in what was maybe not a needed but certainly much wanted breath.

Jessica was watching the harpies without much interest. She wasn't afraid of them and that was the scariest part. She turned back towards me.

"I'm not done with you," she whispered softly. "You're my sister and we're meant to be together, you and me and Jarrod. I won't stop until I get that, Tate. I need this."

176

I cringed as a dark shadow passed over, swept down and drew Jessica away in taloned claws. The bird demon flapped mustard yellow wings and rose, its beak-less face snarling in warning as it passed by. I watched them go. I watched my sister fly away in the arms of a monster and I couldn't have been happier. I crawled over to James and helped Nethel turn him onto his back.

"Please be okay," I whispered aloud as I checked his neck for injuries. There were none, just stitches in a rough line between his shoulder blades and scalp. His eyes fluttered open and he smiled at me, giving me a thumbs up.

"There are perks to this job," he joked as he tried to sit up. I started to cry again. James put his arms around me and apologized. I pulled away from him and looked at the harpies, at the injured demon lying next to us, and then back at the mass of tentacles that was twitching by the goal post behind me.

"We have to find my sister," I said, relief at the harpies' rescue and dread at the impossible task that was looming before me mixing together into one, hard to read emotion. "And we have to do it fast."

James and I released the demons that Jessica had left to their proper places and I found that I knew absolutely nothing about the process that I had thought I was beginning to understand.

"What happened to the dragonfly demon?" I had asked James as Nethel had handed me the bag with the harp. As soon as my fingers had closed around the purse, I had felt a sense of peace. It really was a part of me, just like the flute was a part of Jessica. This was going to make things even harder than I'd thought.

"I released her," James had said with a tight-lipped smile. "To the next life." I raised my eyebrow. His smile had warmed a bit as I'd removed the harp. Apparently, he had known about it all along. He'd just been waiting for me to tell him myself. I felt ashamed. "Some demons are made when a summoner pulls them back from the Library too soon and some," he'd paused and shaken his head. "Some souls are left too long without guidance and they become demons, too. That girl, that 'dragonfly demon,' she'd finished at the Library and been brought back by a summoner. The grim reaper that was supposed to pass her on didn't do his job." Nethel had smiled and helped me to my feet.

"I see you've come up with your own terms, transitioner," she'd said as James wrinkled his nose.

"Transitioner and gatekeep weren't right, too bland. I just spiced it up a bit." I'd wanted to smile at his joke but couldn't; I was drained, emotionally, physically, and spiritually. I had a lot to think about. They'd all gone quiet after that. Nethel and Ehferea had left with a promise to check up on us and get some more information on Jessica's whereabouts. They hadn't mentioned Sydney.

"So," James began as he helped me over the wall. I knew he was just as tired, but I couldn't find the strength to do it myself. "Do you want to hear a story?" He was trying to be lighthearted, but there was a catch in his voice that drew my attention. I straddled the wall and stared down at him.

"What about?" I asked, my voice as dry as bones. I needed to sleep again. Whatever it was, I hoped it could wait. James looked down at his feet and I knew instantly. "Sydney," I said. He nodded. I bit my lip. I wanted, almost needed, to know about Sydney. I felt like it was my first step to understanding and coming to terms with Boyd. I didn't know why, but my gut promised me that. Still, it was going to be emotional and it was going to hurt. I'd had a lot of hurt for one night.

"James," I said, trying to soften my voice, make it sweet as petals. "Let's go home; let's get some sleep. In the morning I – " I couldn't finish my sentence. It was caught in my mouth like peanut butter. I swallowed to clear it. "In the morning, I want you to tell me everything and I … I want to tell you about Boyd."

He looked up at me, his hair reflecting the stars, and held out a hand. I helped him up the wall with a bit of strength I hadn't known I'd had left.

"We're going to make a great team," he said as we paused on the stone wall and stared at each other. I was too hurt to say it out loud, but I thought it.

We already are.

CHAPTER SIXTEEN

I sat on my bedroom floor, flipping through albums that my mother had put together in a hysterical frenzy after my father had died. I'd only been three years old, but I remembered. I could still see the frenzied glint in her eyes and the shimmer of unshed tears. She had plastered picture after picture after picture of Abe and Jessica and Jason and me. I touched a picture of Jessica, sitting on our floral print couch, with a swaddled baby Jason wrapped in her arms. Dad was sitting next to them, smiling down at them like only a parent can do. I barely remembered him at all. I slammed the album shut, coughing at the wave of dust that floated throughout the room, highlighted by the bright bars of sun cutting through the window panes.

I stood up and brushed myself off, carefully replacing the album on the shelf next to a glass clown and a box of arrowheads. I was going to have to go downstairs sooner or later and talk to James. He was going to tell me a story that was going to break my heart and then I was going to have to tell him mine. I checked the time. It was already past noon. I was wasting time that I didn't have. I sighed and unlocked my door.

After we'd come home last night, we had retreated to our respective bedrooms without another word. I'd fallen asleep in my muddy clothes and woke up in the middle of the night itching from stray blades of grass and clumps of dirt. I'd torn the sheets from my bed and changed into another one of my inspiring hoodie-jean outfits. I didn't feel safe sleeping in pajamas. Pajamas were soft and vulnerable and spoke of comfort and home. I didn't have that sense at all anymore.

I paused on the top step and bit my lip. Somebody was cooking. I could smell butter and bacon and very faintly, I could hear the sound of a hot pan sizzling. I took the steps two at a time and found James, complete with one of my grandmother's white lace aprons, at the stove.

"What are you doing?" I asked him, surprised but pleased. I hadn't had anyone cook for me in years, except for Boyd of course. James glanced over his shoulder at me and smiled. His hair was freshly washed and he'd found new clothes to wear. The jeans had been Jessica's, but I was surprised to see how good he looked in them. I tried to grin; I liked guys in girls' pants, but the sadness from last night swept over me at the last moment and stole the happiness from my face. Why, whenever I made progress in my life, did it have to be taken away again?

I sighed and sat down.

"I hope you don't mind me using your kitchen," James said as he turned his attention back to the cooking. "But there wasn't much to eat that didn't need some heating up." I rested my cheek on the tabletop and tried not to stare at his ass. *What the fuck is wrong with you?* I asked myself, guilt and confusion fighting for supremacy. *Your sister tried to kill you last night. For the second time.* I huffed in response to his question and turned my face towards the wall. I wasn't acting like myself and I didn't like it. *That's what happens when you have a revelation,* I told myself. *You change.*

"Make yourself at home," I added when I heard the clatter of plates on the kitchen counter. I hadn't meant it to sound so … bitchy. I raised my head and watched James' face drop. I tapped my fingers on the table and tried to lighten the mood. "Um, did you sleep okay?" I asked in my nicest voice. James nodded but didn't speak. *Is that the best you can do?* "I just wanted to say thank you," I added, hoping that I was making the right decision by bringing up last night. "For saving me." I could still see the knife, reddened with Jessica's blood. I shivered. James smiled again and with the way his stitches stretched and pulled the skin taut against his face, I could tell it was genuine.

"You're welcome," he told me as he lifted the pancake from the pan and presented it to me with a flourish. I smiled back.

"Thanks." James sat down and we ate in silence. The conversion we were supposed to have pushed aside for the moment. We needed to do it, but it was going to be hard. Procrastination seemed like the safest option.

"I was thinking," he said as he finished his food and placed both of our plates in the sink. I expected him to leave them there and was shocked to see him pump pearly soap onto a sponge and lather it up. *What a fucking saint.* "Maybe in a little while we could go out and … " He paused, dried the first plate and placed it on the counter next to him. "Maybe we could find Sydney." I almost choked. He glanced back at me and I nodded.

"Why the change of heart?" I asked him quietly. My heart was pumping so loud I hoped he wouldn't hear it. James finished with the other plate and replaced the apron on the nail by the doorway to the living room. He adjusted the black *Providence High School* sweater he had borrowed and sat down across from me. He reached out his hands and pulled mine closer to him. I let him.

"I want to show you something," he said and I waited in anticipation as he drew a small wallet out from inside the sweater pocket. He opened it with one hand and handed the cracked leather over to me. Inside the plastic covering was a picture of a girl. She had her arm around his waist and grinned back at me from behind a curtain of ebony hair. *This is Sydney.* I swallowed a lump and flipped to the next picture. Sydney, her slanted eyes narrowed suspiciously was dressed in a red cape and a black gown, curling her finger towards the cameraman who I could only assume was James. Next shot, Sydney, asleep on a bus, her pale skin soft in the blush of afternoon light streaming through the window. I closed the wallet and handed it back to him.

"Why are you showing me this?" I asked. James replaced the wallet and squeezed my hands in his.

"Last night, I saw the way she hurt you, Neil." I closed my eyes, but James wouldn't let me. "Look at me, Neil, please. This is hard enough. I have to know that you're here or I can't do it. I've never told anyone else this before." I opened my eyes and watched his fill with tears. He dashed them away with the back of his hand. "I saw your face change the moment you knew she'd put her own interests before yours. I can't do that to Sydney. Keeping her around, following her, just so I can look at a demon that isn't even really her anymore … That isn't love, Neil, and I love her." I nodded but didn't speak. His voice was killing me, ripping me apart, but it was also putting me back together again. It was a painful process.

"Sydney and I have been … " James paused. "*Had* been friends since we were in sixth grade." He grimaced and I could see the use of the past tense was cutting him like a knife. "We were always together. We used to sit together and play Monopoly for hours. She'd never let me stop without finishing the game." James' face started to transform as he talked about his friend. Some of the sadness was slipping away, cloaked in memories. "That was one of the things I liked best about her; she always finished what she started. She was a big xylography fan, too, and she always told me she liked my work, even if I didn't believe she did." I still had no idea what xylography was, but I couldn't bear to interrupt him. His face was blooming like a rose in the spring. Love. That was what love looked like and it was beautiful. I promised myself that I would look it up later. James was rubbing my hands with his thumbs. It was weird at first, to be touched like that, but I decided that it also felt good. I could sense his feelings for Sydney in his touch and I resonated with that.

"Anyway," he continued, nibbling at his stitches and glancing down at the white tiles on the floor. "Things were perfect until we hit high school." He looked up at me sharply and I could see the petals wilting. This is where the story began to sour. "People just couldn't understand that we were only friends. They didn't get that the love we had was special. It wasn't like a girlfriend, boyfriend sort of a thing, some stupid high school fling that gets forgotten like it's nothing. This was special." James ground his teeth at the memory and it was like looking in a mirror. Boyd and I had been like that, but no one got it but us. I squeezed James' hands tighter.

"Or maybe only I saw it like that because Sydney, she … she wanted it to be more, but I just couldn't. It wasn't like that for me. I loved her, but I didn't … you know, I didn't want it to be like that." James watched my face closely, desperate for some sign that I understood. What he didn't realize is that we were the same, me and him. Boyd had loved me like that. I hadn't. It didn't mean I loved him any less, just different. All I could do was nod.

"So I ... " James blushed and pulled his hands back. The silence between us became awkward for the first time since we'd met. Whatever it was he wanted to tell me wasn't going to be easy. *Your story can't be any worse than mine,* I thought with a sudden stab of fear. I was going to have to tell it soon. I was going to have to peel back my ribcage and let him see my heart. As I watched the anxiety swarm across his face, I froze up, promised myself I couldn't do it. *How can he even stand it?* I wondered as he looked pointedly back at me. His eyes were boiling over with determination. He wanted to do it, but it was going to be hard.

"So I had ... so we ... we ... " He waited, hoping I would supply the words, hoping that I would figure it out for myself so he wouldn't have to say it. I waited, my back tense, my spine ramrod straight. What was he trying to say? *Please, don't let it be that.* "So I had sex with her because that's ... that's what she wanted ... " I almost threw up. I almost leaned down and put my head between my legs and emptied my soul on the floor. *Why is he a reflection of my life? How did those fucking harpies know we were the perfect match in misery?* James babbled on, mistaking my silence for judgment. How wrong he was.

"She said it wouldn't mean anything, that she just wanted to try it, that we should be each other's first because we were so close and I ... I should've told her no, but I didn't and then afterward, I felt guilty." James stood and paced across the room to look out the window. I stayed seated, facing towards the living room and away from him. I didn't need to hear the rest; I already knew what happened. I'd seen it myself.

"Things were different then. She was different, I was different and so I started avoiding her … " He trailed off and didn't continue for the longest time. I counted seconds in my head and watched the numbers on the stove move upwards.

"Some of my memories are fuzzy," James whispered softly. "Like they're underwater and I'm looking at them from above, but the day she died, that's as clear to me now as the day I lived it." He leaned over the sink and closed his eyes. "I had just crossed the street towards my house. School had gotten out and I was trying to leave before she saw me. We'd always walked home together, but lately, it hadn't felt right. I think she expected things to change between us, but I just wanted them to go back to the way they were." He whirled around and stared at me, fat drops rolling down his face and neck.

"Do you hate me?" he asked suddenly. I stood up, too, no longer able to sit still.

"No," I whispered, my hands shaking. I understood perfectly. I had to tell him that. He had to know I understood and that there was someone just like him out there in the universe who had made the same mistakes and dealt with the same consequences.

"She called out to me and I ignored her. I pretended I didn't hear," he said and his voice began to quiver, to shake like a bridge in an earthquake. It was trying to stay strong, but when your foundations are struck, you crumble. "She chased after me and I saw it coming. I tried to warn her, but it was just seconds between my voice and the crash. She was so bloody and broken, Neil." James was sobbing now. I went to him like he'd come to me last night and held him while he cried.

"She was bloody and broken and when they took her to the hospital, she never woke up. I can't forget the sound of the metal and the crack of bone on pavement, Neil. It haunts me in my sleep." I shushed him then and brushed his hair back. That was enough. He had told me all I needed to know.

"We'll find her," I whispered, getting the strangest urge to brush a kiss across his forehead. *You're going insane. Grief is making you insane.* I decided against it. "We'll find her and we'll make things better and when she's done at the library, you can say goodbye and you can tell her you're sorry and that you never meant to hurt her and that you love her so fucking much that it kills you inside." I stopped when I realized I wasn't just talking about James. I was talking about myself and Boyd. James pulled away and smiled at me.

"Thanks, Neil," he said as I used my sweatshirt to wipe the tears from his cheeks. "And thanks for being my friend. It takes a pretty brave girl to do that."

CHAPTER SEVENTEEN

"The day that Sydney died, I had the most horrible thoughts about her. I wished she would move away and never come back so that I wouldn't have to watch the hurt in her eyes each and every time she tried to hug me and I pulled away. I told myself that I had only done what she'd wanted because I loved her but in reality, I was being selfish. I wanted us to belong together like that because it made things easier. It made more sense to my mother, to my friends, to the world. But we were never meant to be like that. When I held her that night, I cried because I knew I had made the wrong decision. It meant the world to her and it was only a mistake to me. It was the worst feeling I had ever had. And then she died. Nothing can make that right."

I paused in my reading, realizing that along the way, I had stopped speaking aloud. My lips had failed to keep up with the beat of my heart. I let my lashes rest against my cheek and listened to Boyd play another horrible country song on his grandfather's guitar.

I'd looked everywhere for his ghost. I'd had to, after my talk with James. I folded the letter and tucked it into the front of my jeans. James had showed it to me later, after I'd made him tea and we'd sat in the living room in silence pretending to enjoy a movie that neither of us were watching. I don't know why he'd written it. Maybe he'd thought the words wouldn't be able to escape his throat. Maybe he'd thought they'd clog up in his chest and I'd never know why he was the way he was. Whatever the reason, he'd written it in tiny, careful letters on a piece of Jessica's stationery. I'd swiped it after he'd fallen asleep on the couch and brought it, along with the harp and the pocketknife, here, to the park where Boyd had taught me to play chess.

"I can't stay long," I said as I gazed at the daisies and remembered when James and I had sat under this same tree. It seemed like ages ago but it was only days. I shook my head and relaxed into the grass. The sun cut across my skin in stripes, blocked by thick branches with gold and red and yellow leaves. "I have to go and find Jessica." Boyd didn't answer, of course, but it was nice to lie there and pretend he could, pretend that the song he was playing was just for me and that nothing had gone wrong in the world.

I rolled onto my side and watched the sun reflect

196

off of his balding head. He'd had hair before I'd ruined our relationship. I should've said no. James should've said no. We were one in the same. It was incredible to believe that there was actually someone else in the world that was as fucked up as I was. I closed my eyes and saw the stitches across his brow, across his lower lip, across his throat. His image was burned in my brain and I found that no matter how hard I tried to care about Jessica, all I could think about was James. We had to find her soon, sure, that was obvious, but I had to help James find Sydney. It felt like if I did that, I was one step closer to letting Boyd go. The question was, was I ready to do that?

I picked a daisy, then another, then another until I had a small pile of them clutched against my chest. I'd never made a daisy chain before but I tried, slitting the stems with my thumbnail and weaving them together like James had done. When I was finished, I had a small crown that I presented to Boyd's ghost. I was careful not to touch him. I didn't think I could handle another one of my family members trying to kill me. I stood behind my ghost, ducked down so that I was standing inside of her, mimicking her, and watched Boyd smile at me.

"Did you like it?" He asked, strumming the guitar one last time and placing it in the grass by his side. Ghost Me nodded and I placed the daisy chain between us.

"I liked it so much, I made you this," I said quietly while I heard the other me say something inconsequential, something unimportant. "I should've told you that I loved it, that I knew the songs were always about me and that I cared. I should've told you that I listened to the tapes when I fell asleep and no matter how much I joked about it, I never thought they were creepy." Boyd smiled and laughed. I closed my eyes and followed the Ghost Me to the ground where I lay silently, my knees tucked under my sweatshirt, and listened to him pick up his guitar and start a new song with my eyes closed and the autumn breeze brushing my bangs back from my forehead. For a moment there, things were almost good.

My tranquility was short lived.

A kick to my lower back knocked the air out of me and sent hot waves of pain coursing through the stitches in my belly. I rolled to my feet and came face to face with Margaret Cedar.

"You fucking bitch," she snarled, her usual tight jeans and skimpy tank top replaced with baggy cargo pants and a gray sweatshirt. I stumbled a step back to catch my breath. "You're as much of a freak as that dead sister of yours. They should put your crazy ass in a mental institution or in the ground where you belong." She came at me again, fists swinging wildly. I ducked out of the way of those acrylic pink nails and tried not to think about why she was angry. *She thinks you fucked Jarrod.* I bit my lip and swung back at her, using my anger at Jessica to fuel my punch. When my knuckles connected with her delicate, little jaw, pain bloomed up my arm and made me pause long enough for her to leap at me.

Margaret was a frenzy in glimmer gloss, slapping and pulling and tearing at me like one of the demons I was supposed to banish. I knocked her to her back and tried to get the upper hand by straddling her. By this time, people had begun to stare but nobody was helping. Everyone loves a good fight.

"He's mine, he's mine, he's fucking mine, do you hear me?" I rolled off of her and rose to my feet. She was too wild to hold down, too angry, too fueled by unworthy passion. I pushed her away again and she slammed against the base of the tree with a grunt.

"I don't want to fight you," I said and I meant it. With Jessica, with James, with everything that was going on, my struggle was more internal than external and I didn't think I could handle both. She launched herself forward with a scream of rage. *Love works both ways, Neil, for good and bad.* Boyd had used to say that.

"I always knew you were a whore," she panted, her voice cracking with hysteria and exhaustion. She was wearing herself out and not getting anywhere. She was too hot headed, I was too clear headed, she wasn't getting any shots in and that pissed her off. Verbal abuses poured over my head like rain as I turned to walk away. I could still hear Boyd's country twang but I couldn't enjoy it anymore, not with this. "Is that why he killed himself?" She snarled finally, breaking her vituperative string of curses with one that she knew would hurt the most. "Because you were a shitty lay?" My heart froze in my chest, suspended by her words. *Let it go,* my rational brain begged. *Go home, get James, free Sydney, find Jessica. Those are the things that matter.*

I took a deep breath and continued walking.

"You don't walk away from me," she continued to

screech. "You do not fuck my fucking boyfriend and then walk away from *me*." She barreled into my back, surprising me with the force behind her lanky and as I'd always believed, anorexic, form. I hit the dirt with a thud as she wrapped her hands around my hair and pulled. I tried to throw her off but her frenzy had reached a fervor and her skinny hands were wrapping around my throat, plastic nails raking my skin and drawing blood. I pushed myself up to my elbows and her weight lifted from my back suddenly. I rolled over and found Margaret suspended above me by the beak-less bird.

She screamed, I screamed, and then her head was twisting back at an angle that I knew wasn't right.

This isn't happening, this isn't happening, this isn't happening.

"Jessica, stop!" It was too late. Margaret's limbs were too relaxed, her face too slack, her neck too twisted. Margaret Cedar was dead.

The demon dropped her to the grass in front of me in a heap of adolescent limbs and broken dreams. We used to play Barbies together, we used to eat cut up hot dogs with ketchup and watch cartoons, Jessica used to sleep in the same with bed her on sleepovers. Now, she was dead in front of my feet for a boy that wasn't worth it. *Love works both ways, Neil, for good and bad.* In that moment, I knew his statement couldn't have rung more true.

Screams came to me then from the people in the park. People who had seen the girl who had attacked me die but hadn't seen the bird that killed her. What was I going to do now?

200

"I'm sorry, Neil," Jessica said from behind me. I stumbled to my feet and whirled around to face her. The flute was hanging limply in her right hand. "I meant to kill her before but I wanted her to know first. I'm sorry you had to see it like this." I stared at the girl I had shared a womb with, shared a life, shared deaths.

"Jessica," my tone was firm. I didn't sound scared which was good. I didn't know how to sound scared anymore. Fear implies anxiety at the unknown, trepidation at perceived pain. I was already in the unknown, full of pain. There was nothing left to fear. "Are you trying to ruin what life I have left?" I was going to have to leave Grandma Willa alone in her mansion and travel the country with James with no food and clothes that stank like the sea. *But is that really so bad?* My heart pumped with possibility.

"You belong with me, Neil," she whispered as she lifted the flute to her lips. I reached for the handle of my purse. It wasn't there. Once again, it had been knocked off in a fight. I was going to have to find another way to carry it. I checked the grass. *There, under the tree.* I raced forward and snatched the purse from the ground but before I could even open it, Jessica lips moved across the metal and began to play.

A twang, like Boyd's country music, broke the sweet melody of the flute. I couldn't place the sound at first but it was familiar. I glanced around for the source. Nethel moved into sight from behind a tree, lifted her fingers to her lips and blew. Petals danced in the wind for a moment before swirling, catching the trail of Jessica's music and attaching to her skin like scales. She shrieked in pain and I watched in horror as she changed, from girl to demon. Her hair grew long and full, wrapped her body like a blanket and pulled her to all fours, changed her from my sister into a lion with blue eyes and tails like whips. She roared and the bird demon responded as if summoned. It grasped the flute between its talons and lifted it into the sky, followed by Ehferea who had an arrow, cocked and ready. She released it, skimming the bird's wing and sending it crashing to the ground in a flurry of feathers and tufts of grass.

I caught a movement of blue to my right and turned. There were police officers everywhere, drawn to the park by frantic 911 calls. I was going to go to jail. I paused for a long moment, drawn between the supernatural problems behind me and the civic ones in front. *I can't do this.* My knees shook and I thought I was going to collapse. A strong hand clamped around my arm and spun me to face its owner.

"James," I whispered his name like a dream and fell, forward and down, trying to hold onto some hope but not finding it.

"Let's get out of here," he whispered gently, hoisting me up with Nethel's help and taking me away from the park and the lion that was my sister and the flute she shouldn't have played. I didn't see her take Ehferea, twist her to the ground and snap her neck. I didn't see her take the flute and leave. I'm glad I didn't because even though the harpy got up and walked away as if nothing had happened, I had seen enough death to last me a thousand lifetimes.

CHAPTER EIGHTEEN

J ames took me home and locked the two of us in the pretty bedroom together while Nethel waited outside for Ehferea. As he drew the curtains and I wondered why I still had dry eyes, I realized that this was starting to become his room. Old memories were being replaced with newer, better ones. I tried to smile, but Margaret's death caught at the corners of my lips and drew them down.

"Are you okay?" he asked me as he peeked outside for something, maybe Jessica, maybe a demon, maybe cops. I nodded but didn't speak. He sat down on the unmade bed next to me and wrapped an arm around my shoulder.

"Were you close to her?" he asked, pretending as if he hadn't followed me out there and seen the whole thing though I suspected he might have. When I spoke, my voice was barely above a whisper. Death. Death. Death. I just couldn't escape the inevitable.

"Not anymore." James nodded again and stood up, pacing the length of the room several times before I stopped him with a hand on his arm. "Am I going to jail?" He looked down at me and worried at his stitches.

"I don't know." *At least he's honest.* "But you didn't kill her. They might not have been able to see the demon, but it was obvious that she didn't die by your hands." I stared down at the white and pink floral rug and wondered how long it would take Jessica to find me again. It wasn't like I was in hiding. She had lived here, too. She would come, eventually. A knock at the door interrupted our silence. James and I exchanged worried glances.

He tiptoed to the door and leaned his ear against it. I followed suit.

The old doors creaked open and Grandma Willa answered.

"How can I help you boys?" she asked in her afternoon-medication voice, the one where she got all foggy and far away. I frowned. *Had she seen us come in?* I tried to think. She had. She absolutely had. I grit my teeth and prepared to make a run for it. I could get out the window and down the street before the cops even knew what was happening and if they shot me, what the hell would happen? More stitches? James placed a hand on my arm.

"She isn't here," I heard Grandma Willa saying. "She went to school this morning and hasn't been back? Is there a problem?" *She was covering for me. Grandma Willa could barely remember that I existed and she was covering for me.* Thank you, I whispered in my heart. I would tell her later, I promised myself that. I would tell her I loved her, too. I hadn't said it in a long time, but deep down, I knew it was true.

James straightened back up and went to the curtains. He pulled the lace aside and waited until the cops had gotten back in their car and left before speaking.

"We have to find Jessica," he said, turning to face me again with a grim face. "We have to find her and send her on before she kills anybody else. I'm starting to wonder if we should be worried about that guy, what's his name, the red head?" I sighed. He was right. Jarrod. We had to find Jarrod and protect him from Jessica though I almost felt like it was a waste of life. He should've died and not Margaret. How could Jessica be so selfish?

"I can show you where he lives?" I suggested, absolutely determined not to go back to the school or the park. If he wasn't there, too bad, his loss. "It's getting late, he should be home by now."

That is, if my sister hasn't already killed him.

I walked to Jarrod's house in a daze. Margaret was dead, she wasn't my favorite person, that was fine, but I'd had enough. I stopped James with a hand on his elbow. He paused but didn't look at me. We still hadn't exactly addressed the Sydney issue and I think, but I wasn't positive, that he was embarrassed.

"Thanks for telling me," I said. I didn't need to specify. James knew what I was talking about. He kept his gaze on the sidewalk as I glanced over my shoulder at Nethel. She had agreed to follow us at a distance though I wouldn't say discreetly. She wasn't more than ten steps away. "And after this, I think we should go and find her." James swallowed and nodded. He knew it was the right thing, but it was going to be difficult. I wished I could give him courage, but I was having trouble finding my own. I glanced back down at him and watched the waning sunlight play off of his hair. I needed to show him something that let him know that I was here. *We're the same, you and me. We lived identical lives with different people in different places and we understand each other. I get it, James, I get it.*

I said nothing and kept walking.

Before we even got to Jarrod's house, I knew there was a problem.

The front door was missing.

James and I paused, glancing at one another and then back at Nethel for confirmation. Ehferea still hadn't come back yet and if I really was starting to get a hang of how the stoic harpies thought, I would say that Nethel was worried. She stepped between us and went into the house without stopping. James and I waited for her in silence. When she reappeared, I expected her white feathers to be coated in blood. I just expected death all the time now. Sad. When she came out, though, she was still as white as a pearl, glimmering and changing tones in the light.

"Jarrod is not present though it appears it has not been long since he was here. Shall I search the area for him?" Nethel looked up at the sky, her dark eyes searching for her partner. I followed her gaze but found nothing but white clouds and the telltale oranges and red of evening peeking over the edges of the mountaintops. I adjusted my sweatshirt to ward off the coming chill. It might've just been the weather or maybe I was starting to get paranoid. I swore I could feel Jessica's eyes boring into my back. I turned around and found nothing.

"Well," James began. "I guess that would be best. If he's still around here, we need to find him before Jessica … " He trailed off. He didn't need to state the obvious and he knew it.

"Very well," Nethel confirmed, raising her wings. "I will report back to you in this vicinity. Do not wander too far."

When she was gone, James and I were left standing awkwardly on a sidewalk with no discernible direction. I wished suddenly that there was a compass pointing us in the right direction. *Do we find Sydney? Do we wait here? Do we look for Jessica?* I turned around and went up the stairs. I had to do *something*. James followed me soundlessly into the apartment.

As far as I knew, Jarrod lived here with his bitch of a mother who cared more about poker tournaments and fucking their players than she did about her own son. No wonder Jarrod was such an asshole.

The house was ransacked. Pictures were smashed

on the floor, tables were overturned, the TV was a smoking mass of melted plastic on the carpet. I let my mind put together a picture of what it would've looked like beforehand and it wasn't much better. Those holes in the walls looked like they'd been there for quite some time and the dirty carpet and crooked kitchen cabinets didn't look new either. Jessica's demons had done a lot of physical damage, but signs of emotional stress were everywhere.

"How depressing." I wasn't sure if James had said it or if I had. I put my sweatshirt hood over my hair and pulled the drawstrings tight. I couldn't have agreed more either way.

"This is the price of love, huh?" I asked him. He jumped as if he'd been stung by a jellyfish. The look he threw my way was less than pleasant. He looked ... disappointed.

"Love?" he asked, adjusting Jessica's sweatshirt and tugging on the loops of her pants to keep them from riding down. "This isn't about love. This about control. This is about taking something from someone that they weren't willing to give you freely in the first place." I kicked over a broken chair and neglected to respond. What was I supposed to say to that? "Love is perfect and gentle and it doesn't take, it only gives." I looked at James as he spoke. His face was less pale, more passionate. Here was a person who knew what he was talking about. James had loved Sydney. Period. I glanced away, ashamed for disagreeing but unable to control the cynicism that dripped from my lips like poison. Had I learned nothing?

"It seems more like a punishment. I mean, look at

us, we loved and look where we're at now?" I gestured at the apartment. "We're dead and we can't see the ones we would've died for. We have to send them on and we have to stay here. That doesn't seem very gentle or perfect or amazing to me. If what I've been through isn't a punishment, then I don't know what is."

Nethel's feathered feet were so quiet on the floor that neither of us heard her come in.

"This isn't a punishment," she said, her voice like the drip of rain in a spring puddle, soft, soothing, melodic. "You two were chosen for a reason. At the time of your deaths, you loved more purely, more fully than most people will ever understand. They go to the Library to try and determine the meaning of life. You have already found it. Who better to assist them in their journey than you?" I turned around and stared at her, just stared at her. I was a walking indeterminate, unlife *thing* because I loved too much? I didn't speak. I was mad, pissed, but James, he looked happy and I think he even had a tear at the corner of his eye. I was instantly jealous. Why couldn't I believe in all of the happy, flowery, puppies and kittens type stuff, too?

"But ... " My voice trailed off as I thought of Boyd. Love. True love. I had felt it for him, sure. But it hadn't been romantic. Had that been good enough? I had loved him with all of my soul. I would've died for him. That was the meaning of life? I shook my head. It was hard to buy that. "But when will we die? When do we get to move on and forget the hurt? Because that's the price you pay for love, and I'm just about tapped out." I tried to make it funny, but it just sounded sad.

"It's not up to us," Nethel replied, folding her wings behind her and swinging her gaze over the trashed apartment. "Ehferea and I, the harpies, we are here because we have failed time and time again to understand. This is our punishment." I blinked back at her. That was the most information I'd gotten out of them yet. It wasn't much, but it was a start. "But isn't the reward worth the price?"

"It's worth any price." The words blurted from my mouth before I could stop them. Nethel and James both smiled warmly at me. I turned away and pretended to cough. There it was. I did have a revelation. I was making progress. It was actually pretty embarrassing. All of my life, I'd worn the cloak of anger and cynicism and frustration. Now, I was showing my skin and it was tougher than I'd thought. I kicked at a half empty beer can and watched it roll foam and gold liquid across the rug. "Any sign of Jessica?" I asked, trying to pretend that my previous statement had meant nothing when, in reality, it had meant everything. Nethel's feathers ruffled as she shook her head. The smile faded from her yellow lips and she stepped back into the doorway, watching cars idle up and down the quiet street. In this part of town, nobody even noticed or cared about a missing front door.

"She has fled to the Library with Ehferea at her back. We must wait. We cannot track her there." My heart thumped painfully in my chest. The Akashic Library. I wanted to go there. Since James had first told me about it at the restaurant, I had wanted to go. Boyd would be there. I could talk to him. I could tell him my problems like I always had and he would tell me what to do. I decided that it wouldn't hurt to ask.

"Why not?" James placed a hand on my shoulder. Nethel wasn't answering me, just letting the breeze blow her feathered hair back from her swan like neck and taking slow, shallow breaths of the evening air.

"We can't go there, Neil, not yet." I challenged him with my eyes.

"Why?" I asked as he joined Nethel by the front door. It was obvious that he knew more than he was letting on. I wouldn't have even been surprised to learn that he'd been there. "If Jarrod's there, we need to follow her and get him back."

"Jarrod is not there," Nethel replied quietly. James turned around, his face ashen.

"Because he's coming down the street towards us." I stumbled to the door, tripping over empty alcohol bottles and a broken vase full of moldy flowers. It was Jarrod all right. He hadn't seen the missing front door yet. His head was down and a scarf was wrapped across his neck so that it covered nearly half of his face. From his somber appearance, I was guessing that he knew about Margaret.

"We have to get out of here," I said, my hand at my throat. If he found me in his trashed house and called the police, I was screwed. James nodded and we retreated to the sliding glass doors at the back of the living room. Nethel followed us and we closed the door slowly behind us. The backyard was really just a patch of dead grass with a short, chain link fence. We let ourselves out and retreated down the back alley and into the parking lot of a neighboring complex. I breathed a sigh of relief and peeped around the corner for any signs that Jarrod had seen us. There was nothing.

"I've been thinking," James began slowly. His voice was so low that both Nethel and I leaned forward to hear. "Jessica is, as of right now, priority one, of course, but we can't follow her to the Library. She has more power there, as a spirit. We'd be less than helpless, our instruments won't even work there so we won't be able to send her on and I … " He trailed off and spun on his heel to face me. His navy eyes were bright with passion as he gripped my shoulders softly. "Will you help me?" he pleaded, his gaze boring into mine. He recognized that kinship between us even if he didn't know exactly why it was there. I was going to have to tell him soon. I was going to have to spill my guts and lay them across the floor for him to see. I swallowed painfully. "I've been selfish. I want to find Sydney; I want to save her." When I looked over at Nethel, was smiling.

"Yes," I whispered back softly, knowing this was a painful first step for both us. "I was hoping you would say that."

CHAPTER NINETEEN

J ames kept up his determination as Nethel led us down back alleys and along streets I'd never walked. We were taking a roundabout way to the house to avoid cops, students, anyone that knew anything about the death of Margaret Cedar or the trashing of Jarrod's house. To get to where Sydney was now, Nethel had told us we'd need the car. James hadn't liked that. His face had drooped and in his eyes, I had seen the pain and the fear and the loss hit him like a freight train.

I kept my eyes on the cracks in the pavement and tried not to notice. It wasn't that I didn't want to comfort him, but I was starting to remember, too. His eyes, the way his hands shook, his memories, they were like a strong breeze, stirring up my own memories like the autumn leaves that littered our front yard. I was trying my best to rake them all back together. I squeezed my eyes shut against images of bloody carpets and slit throats and opened them to the house. Anita was in the garden watching the two of us suspiciously. Not good.

"I'll get the keys," I whispered as I raced up the front steps and inside. Anita didn't stop me, but her eyes followed me, boring into my spine and making me stumble. This wasn't right. I didn't want to be blamed for causing pain to anyone. When we left, I was going to make a point to drive the long way around the block, away from Margaret's house and her grieving family.

I grabbed the keys from the bowl and found Grandma Willa watching me from the living room.

"Going out?" she asked and I could tell from her voice that she was back, at least for the moment. I nodded but didn't speak. My throat was too dry. *Jessica's made it hard for you to come back here. You don't know how long it will be. You don't know what will happen. Tell her now, Neil. Life is short.* "Be careful, Neil," she said. I turned away and placed my hand on the doorknob. My heart was on fire. *Now or never, Neil. It's now or never.* I spun back around.

"Grandma Willa," I said. She put her knitting down and folded her hands in her lap. "Thanks for everything and I … " The words stuck in my throat, refused to come out. The blood was still running freely from my wounds and only I could apply the first bandage. "I love you." Her face lit up and just like that, I knew I'd made a difference in not only myself but in her, too.

218

"I love you, too, Neil." We smiled at each other for a moment and then she said, as if she knew exactly what was going on, "Run along now and do what you have to do." I nodded and turned around, letting my hand linger on the doorknob before leaving. *Even if I never get to come back, even if Jessica has ruined this for me, there will be something else and it'll be okay. I know it will.*

I pushed the door open and found James with his hands tucked nervously behind his back. Nethel was waiting for us at the end of the driveway and Anita was pruning the roses angrily. *Snip. Snip. Snip.* She was acting as if they'd personally offended her. When she saw the keys in my hands, her eyes widened.

"You don't have a license," she said, pausing, her green clippers holding a half severed branch hostage. *Defuse the situation, now.* I took a deep breath and smiled at her, really smiled, let my feelings for my grandmother come out through my lips.

"I don't," I said, purposely reaching for James' hand and pressing the metal against his cold skin. *Is mine that cold now, too?* I didn't have time to speculate. Proof of my own demise was a little hard to swallow. It was something I was going to have to deal with later. James bit down on his own lip, blood spilled, trickled down his chin and dripped to stain the darkness of his sweater. He ran his hand across his face, red smearing the back of his pale hand and I noticed with surprise that there was already an extra X on the front of his lip. "But my friend, James, does. You haven't met James yet, have you, Anita?" She shook her head and the suspicion in her eyes lifted, at

219

least a little. I couldn't tell if she had heard about the park incident, or if there was something else. We couldn't stay long enough to find out.

"Nice to meet you, James," she said, the clippers closing finally and releasing the branch from its misery. He nodded and grumbled something under his breath.

"I see what you're doing," he said, leaning over and whispering to me. "But I can't drive. I *can't*, Neil." I kept smiling at Anita and started to drag him towards the Seville. I threw my hood up and tucked my hair back before grasping him gently by the forearms.

"You can," I said and then paused. I watched the sun reflecting off of an oil spot on the driveway. It looked dark at first, black, but when the sun hit it just right, there were all of the colors in the rainbow. Life was like that. Things might seem bleak, but sometimes, sometimes there were hidden colors. I smiled. I was starting to sound like Abe. My inner cynic roared protest and I pushed it back. I met James' eyes. "Do it for Sydney." James didn't move for a moment and my heart stopped beating. Had I gone too far?

He closed his fist, squeezing the keys in his hand for a moment before putting them to the lock. A grin whispered up from my chest and took over my face. I was proud of him and I couldn't help but show it.

"Let's go get her," he whispered as I closed the passenger door behind me. "Let's go free Sydney."

Nethel guided us from the air, her pale body shimmering like the inside of an abalone shell. First, she was pink, then yellow, then blue. I leaned forward, hands on the dashboard and watched her massive wings carry her over trees and under power lines. I sat back and checked James out from the corner of my eye. He was trembling and worrying at his lip again. Blood was trickling freely now. I reached over and pressed my hand across his mouth. His eyes slid to mine for just a second before snapping back to the road.

"Stop," I said. I was getting better at disassociating the sight of blood with my memories, but I wasn't perfect. I folded my sweatshirt over my hand and wiped the red away. James didn't protest, but he didn't look at me again, either. His eyes were stuck to the road like they were glued there. I slumped back in my seat and watched Nethel turn sharply towards the right, down an alley. James came to a complete stop, flicking on the blinker and practically rolling into the narrow lane.

"You drive like an old person," I said, trying to make a joke and avoiding the blood stain on my sleeve. James had a real reason to be scared. His phobia was perfectly justifiable and, considering we were on our way to send Sydney to the Library, he was bound to be upset, but I felt like I had to try.

"Do you like baseball?" he asked me. I turned to him with a raised eyebrow. He was back to his anxious babbling. I smiled softly. Of all the types of nervous ticks to have ... At least I could get some information out of him.

"Do I look like the kind of person that enjoys competitive sports?" James tried to smile, bless his little, black heart, he really did, but it came out more as a grimace. I tried to lighten the mood. "I like chess. Oh, and origami. Paper cranes are my secret love interests. You?" James slammed on the brakes, sending us both straining against the confines of our seat belts. When I looked up, I saw that we had turned out of the alley and were at a stoplight. The light was still yellow.

"Baseball's okay, I guess," he continued, as if nothing had happened. I doubted that he was really conscious of what he was saying. His eyes told me he was thinking about one thing and one thing only. Sydney. "I don't really know much about it, but my friends were all into it so I've seen some games." I smiled back and tried not to think of Jessica and the baseball player she'd dated right before she died. This wasn't her time. This was mine and James' and then it was going to be James' and Sydney's. Later, I would dig deeper and try to uncover the land mine she'd placed inside my heart. Right now, it was dormant. "But you know what's really great?" He asked, his tone unbelievably upbeat. It was a good act, but still, that's all it was. An act. "Figure skating. Figure skating has got to be my favorite Olympic sport."

"James," I interrupted. I didn't want to be rude, but I was starting to get worried. The more he talked, the lighter his tone became and the more his hands tightened around the steering wheel. I tried to keep my tone light, but I wanted him to know I was serious.

"Are you going to be okay? Because if you're not, I'm not letting you go. Do you understand?" Silence reigned king for a moment. I reached into the center console and pulled out a pack of gum. I tried to hand him a piece, but he waved it away.

"I'm ready," he whispered slowly as the trees outside the window cast shadows across his pale face. "And I know she's more than ready. That's what counts." I nodded and we drove the rest of the way without speaking again. I wondered if I'd made a mistake, but I felt in my heart that I had to ask. Sydney deserved better. I'd needed James to help me with Jessica. Today, I would help him.

After a twisting maze of side streets and a dirt road that led to nowhere, we came to a stop outside of a rusted fence with a missing gate and a busted padlock hanging from a hole in the chain link. Nethel circled, like a massive eagle honing in on her pray, and landed on the ground next to the car. I opened my door tentatively as James set the emergency brake and was glad that I still had the pocketknife in my boot. This looked like the kind of area where thugs were more of a worry than demons. Looking around, I had no clue where we were at. I tried to ask Nethel, but her gaze was directed elsewhere.

"I must attend to Ehferea," she replied cryptically, in a voice devoid of emotion. "I will return." She folded her wings behind her and paused, glancing at James who was gazing past the fence and down a trail. Her face tightened for a brief moment with worry. She leaned in and brushed her strange, yellow lips across my ear. "He must do this. It is absolutely vital to the healing of his soul." When she stood back up, her face was clean, like a whiteboard, erased. James turned back around, his eyes partially glazed over. Nethel didn't even need to whisper. He wouldn't have heard her anyway. She smiled at him briefly, tenderness evident in her gaze, and left in a swirl of dust. James blinked like he was coming out of a trance and tried to smile at me.

"Ready?" he said and I could only wonder if he were asking me or himself. I watched his face for signs of distress or regret, but there was only sadness. I decided to keep him in my field of vision at all times. Talking was one thing, doing was another.

Without any further clues from the harpies, we were left to wander the area alone. There wasn't much to find though, just an abandoned house that was really more like a shack and lots and lots of garbage. People had apparently been using this area as a dumping ground for mattresses, TVs, barbeques and a whole lot of refrigerator parts. White doors lay on top of old washers and dryers and made it hard for me to see the demon sleeping among them. James spotted her first.

"There she is," he whispered as my hand touched the bag with my harp for reassurance. It was comforting to know it was there even if I knew it wouldn't help in this situation. I pulled the strap from my shoulder and threaded it through my belt loop and then back through itself to make a knot. Things had gotten messy before. They were bound to be messy again. I didn't want to lose the harp this time. I tugged on the bag to make sure it was secure and nodded at James to continue. I hadn't officially introduced him to the harp yet, but I would, after this was all over.

"How do we get to her?" I asked, examining the minefield of garbage. There was no way I was crawling over all of that. Sydney would hear us, if she hadn't already, and I'd be helpless, mired in trash. At the warehouse, she'd acted as if she were ready to move on, but then, she was a demon. I didn't want to take any chances. I reached down and grasped James' shaking hand. He squeezed mine back so hard it hurt. I had to make this as painless as possible for him. No heroics, no acrobatics, no drama. I took a deep breath and pulled him around the pit, searching the landscape and my own brain for an idea.

The fact that Jessica was still running around out there somewhere, gunning for me, made my hands itch. Reflexively, I reached towards my back pocket for the imaginary Glock. I couldn't wait until I was old enough to buy a real one. I released James' hand and knelt down, looking for something to throw. I was going to have to wake Sydney up and get her to come over to us. It seemed like the most logical option.

"Neil," James choked out. I glanced up and found that Sydney was already awake. She was watching us with dark eyes, like endless pools. Again, I was struck with that connection between us. Sydney understood me. She was watching me with expectance and a high level of intelligence that belied what I already knew about demons. Sydney knew we were there to help. I rose slowly, trying not to startle either her or James.

"Sydney," I called out. My voice rang across the emptiness and echoed back at me. *Sydney, Sydney, Sydney.* "Are you ready?" She rose to her feet, her

225

hooves catching on the mattress she'd been sleeping on, and stumbled. James tried to rush forward and I held him back. His body stiffened, but he complied. Just like I'd known to listen to him with Jessica, he understood that I knew best in this situation. "Are you going to let me do it this time?" I asked him, the stitch in my forehead twinging in remembrance. James grunted but didn't speak. His eyes were all for her.

Sydney crawled through the dump at an agonizing pace and I had to wonder why she'd gone out there in the first place when I noticed the blood on her back leg. The mattress had been so stained that I hadn't thought to connect the pink tinge to the demon. That's why she was stumbling. James noticed it too and I felt his mental distress rain down on me like a thunderstorm.

I grabbed his hand and pulled him around the pit so that I could get a better look. Sydney's leg injury looked an awful lot like Nethel's back wound. I choked on my saliva and had to cough several times before I could catch my breath.

Jessica.

"Wait!" I called out, but Sydney wasn't listening. She was pulling against a rusted car door that had tangled in her raven hair, bucking and slashing her antlers through the air in distress.

There was something out there. I hadn't noticed before, but now I could feel it. Eyes. There were eyes boring into my spine like needles. I turned to James. He was so focused on Sydney that I had to shake him to get his attention.

"Try and stop her," I said as his face registered confusion. "Just trust me," I added, using the words

226

he'd thrown at me when he'd told me to touch the red demon. "I'll explain later." I checked the harp once more to make sure that I'd have easy access to it and ran towards the trees. It might not have been the smartest thing to do. Maybe I was wrong, maybe the demon I was after wasn't Jessica and I was going to get myself mauled. I decided to trust my gut and vaulted over an old bicycle and into the darkness of the forest.

Trash littered the ground here, too. There were so many old cars, wrapped in ivy, that at first, I thought they were a series of small hills. I kicked a headlight out of my way and kept my eyes open, my fingers poised on the strings of the harp. I thought about playing it, just in case, but I didn't want to blow my cover. Jessica didn't know about the harp yet. Once she did, she would be more cautious. I had to catch her off guard.

"Jessie?" I called, using her childhood nickname. She'd hated it as much as I'd hated Tattle, but I thought it was worth a try. I wanted her attention directed at me, not Sydney. She was trying to get back at James. I just knew it.

"You're choosing him over me?!"

I cringed at the memory and tried not to feel guilty. I hadn't done anything wrong. Jessica had. She'd left me alone with no one when she'd killed herself. She'd taken my life, selfishly, and now, she was trying to do it again, to take my soul and bind it with her flute. She was the one who needed a good, old fashioned guilt trip. I swallowed and tried again. "Jessie?"

A low rumble reverberated through the trees. I stepped back and looked up, trying to find the source of the noise. All I could see were the tangled limbs of trees and little blocks of sunshine streaming through the foliage and dappling the dirty cars and black garbage bags with beautiful light.

"Jessica?" Another crash sounded behind me and I jumped, spinning around and expecting to find a lion or a girl, someone with my sister's eyes. Instead, it was Ehferea, dark and beautiful, like a crumpled raven. I stumbled over an abandoned computer tower and knelt at her side. The symbolism of finding her, warm but unmoving, just like the crow, wasn't lost on me. I swallowed and tilted her sharp chin towards me. Her eyes were open and blazing. I tried to jerk back, but she grabbed my wrist with her sharp nails, black talons digging into my skin and making me bleed.

"She is here, tread carefully." And then she was standing and loading her bow like nothing had happened. But I could see blood now, on her wings, in her hair, it glittered like rubies against the blackness of her feathers. She lifted the glowing bow, the dark and silver flame of her arrow highlighting the deep curves of her cheekbones, and shot, I thought, blindly into the trees.

There was a screech, like that of a dying falcon, and the yellow beak-less bird smashed through the foliage, feathers exploding outwards like a sun burst, and crashed right through the roof of a rusted orange sedan.

"Please, do not approach it. She requires a transitioner's touch." Ehferea turned away and started back towards the garbage dump. I chased after her, my eyes tracking the movements of the bird demon. It was flailing and screaming, wings bursting through the windows of the car, while blood leaked down the rusted metal and sank into the dirt. I glanced away, at Ehferea's back.

"Where is she?" I asked, struggling to catch up. Ehferea paused and turned back towards me.

"I cannot track her precise location. She has stolen several artifacts from the Library. One of these is known as the soul tracker. Ironically, it actually interferes with my ability to locate Ms. O'Neil." I raised an eyebrow. If I wasn't mistaken, the stoic harpy had just used sarcasm. "Please be careful," she said, reaching out and brushing her nails over my cheek. It was a light touch, almost affectionate. "She also has possession of a weapon that is able to wound my immortal flesh. I am afraid I cannot be as helpful to you as I would like."

"Who are you?" I asked suddenly. I still knew almost nothing about the harpies. Ehferea smiled sardonically and turned away. I chased her into the clearing but couldn't force another question past my lips. What I saw nearly broke my heart.

Sydney was lying on her side in the dirt. James hadn't been able to stop her from climbing out of the pit, but they were okay with Nethel standing guard over them. He was crying, softly, like only adults can. It was one of those sad, soft sobs that I recognized from my own experiences. He held her head in his lap, his hands tangled in her mess of dark hair, one hand stroking along her face, comforting her. There was blood everywhere, all over her white fur and pooling around her like a black mirror. She had strained herself climbing out of the dump and I had to choke back my own tears. I had to be strong for James. I couldn't blame myself for Jessica's actions.

"James?" I approached him carefully and slid my arms around his neck before kneeling down and pressing myself along his back. Comfort. Friendship. He needed it now more than ever. "Are you ready?" He didn't respond, just kept stroking Sydney's face and whispering a million things he was going to have to repeat when she came back from the Library. She didn't understand what he was saying. She was smart, for a demon, and in some way, she recognized him, but he was wasting his beautiful words. "James?"

"I didn't mean to leave like that. That morning, I just … " He rubbed his arm across his face and knelt forward, planting a kiss on her forehead, between her antlers. "I was just confused. If I could go back, I'd do it different. I'd do everything right by you, Sydney. I'd take back the hurt and the pain. I love you, Sydney, and I'm so sorry. I am so fucking sorry … "

"He must hurry," Ehferea whispered, her eyes scanning the tree line. "I believe your sister is coming."

I scooted forward on my knees and grabbed James' face in my hands. I could feel that needling against my spine again. I had been right. That was her.

"James?" I asked again. His eyes were glazed over with memories, but he nodded slowly. "Are you ready?" He tried to pull away from me, but I held him tight, the tips of my fingers digging into his skin. James shut his eyes and fat tears squeezed under his lids, traced across my skin, light as feathers. "When I read a book that I like, I cut the cover off and tack it to the walls of my bedroom." James opened his eyes and stared at me. This is how he'd done it, how he'd calmed me before. It had worked brilliantly. "My oldest brother, Abe, was sixteen when I was born. My mother was already six months pregnant with him when she turned fifteen, but her and my dad, they were soul mates so it was okay. That's how I knew I loved Boyd but that I wasn't in love with him. I didn't look at him the same way my mom looked at my dad. Does that make any sense at all?"

James had stopped crying.

He reached his hands up and covered mine.

"Sydney's favorite color is purple and she hates the rain because it looks like the sky is melting. She thinks the English language is the best one on earth because there are so many words to choose from, but she says that her native language, Japanese, is prettier when it's written because there are so many characters … " I smiled and placed that gentle kiss on his forehead that I'd been wanting to give him since the kitchen.

"I'll take good care of her," I promised him as he moved back and let me place Sydney's head in my own lap. It was an honor to be trusted like that.

"I wouldn't let anyone else touch her," he told me. "Somehow, I knew deep down that I was waiting for you." I smiled as tears stung my own eyes and glanced down at Sydney. I was so focused on her that I didn't see Jessica, human once again, watching me from the safety of the trees.

"Sydney," I began, gazing into those dark pools and seeing myself reflected back at me. "Are you ready?" She didn't nod, she didn't even really move, but there was this imperceptible shift in her demeanor, like she was preparing for something. I took a deep breath and pressed my fingers against her forehead. "And I'm sorry about my sister," I whispered as her body began to fade, leaving my lap empty and cold.

"No worries," came a voice, soft and gentle, like snowflakes against a roof. You couldn't really hear them, but you knew they were there. "Take care of him." Soft lips brushed my forehead, smooth and sweet, and then she was gone. I sat, stunned for a moment at the connection I'd felt with Sydney. We would've been friends, I just knew it. I gathered my courage and glanced over at James, expecting sadness, despair, maybe even regret.

But there was none of that.

He was smiling the most radiant smile I had ever seen on that beautifully scarred face.

"You set her free," he told me with tears running across his lips and dripping down his chin. "You set *us* free." I brushed the hair from his face and pressed my forehead against his. "Thank you," he whispered finally. I nodded and used my thumbs to brush his tears away.

Nethel and Ehferea approached us slowly, pausing a respectable distance away. At first, I thought they were going to warn us about Jessica. I could still feel her eyes on my back, but this was James' time. He needed this. My sister would have to wait.

"Tatum." It was Ehferea. Her voice was still beautiful, still mystical and alluring, but there was a hint of strain there. "It's time." James and I looked up at her, confusion mirrored in both our faces.

232

"We have another assignment for you," Nethel began and I almost choked. In her pale hand was a piece of paper and on it, an address that I recognized better than my own.

Boyd.

It was my turn to say goodbye.

I wilted, like a flower, into James.

You're being selfish, I told myself. *This is his time. You* know *that.*

"Why now?" I asked, feeling as if our beautiful moment had been taken from us. "Why couldn't you have waited. I … " James put a finger to my lips.

"These things can't wait, Tate." I didn't correct him about my name. Neil was Boyd's nickname for me anyway. Maybe James wanted his own identity as my friend. "If you love something, you have to let it go. I should've let Sydney go sooner and then … " He glanced at the pool of blood. I swallowed and nodded, blinking back fresh tears. I would do this. I had to do this.

I tilted my head back and looked at the sky. First, there was something I wanted to do.

James was sharing so much of himself with me, I would do the same.

"Come with me," I said, rising and pulling him to his feet. "I want to show you something."

CHAPTER TWENTY

I paused in the doorway for a moment, blocking James' view of my room. The crows laughed back at me with their silent faces. *You are a freak. You always will be. Boyd was the only person left that loved you. Nobody else ever will.* I steeled myself for rejection and moved aside. It was now or never. James had shared his story with me and we'd said goodbye to Sydney together. I wasn't ready to tell him about Boyd yet, but I could at least share this. This dirty, wicked, twisted part of me.

"As you can see," I said as I gestured lamely at my collection. "I'm the perfect grim reaper. I've always had this thing for death." James stepped into the attic slowly with a look of wonder on his face, like he was entering another world. I just couldn't tell if he was pleased to be there or not. I sat on the edge of my unmade bed and plucked at the fraying edges of an old quilt I'd found in one of the trunks. He approached the crows first and brushed his fingers across the feathers on their sleek, black heads. His cheeks were still wet with tears, but he wasn't crying anymore. My heart went out to him.

"Why?" he asked. I'd never had anyone ask me that before. Not even Boyd. Boyd had just accepted me the way I was. James, though I think he did accept me, liked to understand why, to dig beneath the surface for more. I wasn't sure which was better.

"You know," I said, wetting my lips with my tongue. I'd never told anyone this before, but if I'd learned anything in the past couple of days, it was that life was temporary. There wasn't time to hold anything back. If I didn't say what I wanted to say now, if I didn't express myself and come clean with who I really was, then I might never get the chance to. "There are only a few perfect moments of real death." I paused again and took a deep breath. James kept his gaze on my collection. "Where you're no longer you, but you're not someone else either." My last statement caused him to turn around. He watched me with dark eyes, the shafts of moonlight through the window highlighting the stitches around his lips. "Before the flies come, before the people, the fire, whatever because when they do, you're not you anymore but something else and I ... " Sadness hit me like a wrecking ball. I doubled over, my heart still pounding a painful requiem in my chest. "And I just wanted to stop that." Tears fell and splashed against my bare knees.

Mom. Dad. Jason. Abe. Boyd.

"I wanted to prolong that moment forever and I ... " James wrapped his arms around my head and pulled me against his chest. I didn't return the hug, but I let him hold me. It was nice to be held by someone, to be loved by someone.

Does James love me?

I pushed that thought away. I wasn't ready for that. I might never be ready for that again.

"I just wanted them to have what everyone else in my life couldn't. A second chance." James released me and stepped back.

"That's why we have to help. It's why we're here, to make sure that everyone gets a second chance." There was no trace of sadness in his voice, but I knew he had to still be thinking about Sydney. I nodded, using the end of his sweater to dry my eyes. I knew what I had to do, with Boyd, with Jessica. I just didn't want to do it.

"Will she hate me?" I asked him. James released me and stepped back, pushing his hair away from his face. I studied him in the moonlight, silhouetted against the backdrop of my bedroom and I decided that maybe, just a little, he was starting to become handsome to me. Or maybe he had been all along and I just hadn't noticed. I decided that I even liked the stitches on his lip.

"I don't know," he replied honestly. "But I know you'll hate yourself if you don't do it. She isn't mired here by love, like you and me." I almost blushed. I'd never blushed in my whole life and now I was feeling

heat in my cheeks? It was wildly inappropriate. "She's letting herself be held here by hate. We can save her from that, Neil." I bit my lip and tried to be strong. James had let Sydney go. It had hurt, but he'd done it. He'd loved her enough to let her go. I had to do that for Boyd and for Jessica. I looked up at him, trying to project the strength that was starting to build in my heart into my voice.

"Let's do it."

The harpies had disappeared again, presumably to search for Jessica, leaving James and I on our own. I decided to take the car although I knew it wasn't fair to James. I just didn't think my legs would carry me there, along that same path that had only led to pain. Unfortunately, the drive didn't help. By the time we reached the trailer, my entire body was shaking like I was in the throws of a fever. My newfound confidence had dropped off about halfway back, stranded on the side of the ride, lost, abandoned. I was going to have to see Boyd dead again, sprawled out across the floor of the trailer like a wasted dream. I bit my lip until I drew blood and a small stitch appeared over the wound. I nibbled at the thread with my teeth as I sat in the passenger seat and wished I could thank James for driving me. His hands were still corpse stiff, clenched around the steering wheel for dear life, his face drenched with a nervous sweat.

"It's gonna be okay, Neil," he whispered, prying his fingers off of the car and placing them gently around mine. I nodded and tried to believe that. I tried to remind myself that this was the right thing to do. Boyd deserved to move on. He was selfless and had always, always, always put his problems on the back burner for mine. It was time to switch things up.

"Let's go," I choked out, tearing my hand away and stepping out of the car. I hoped the Orangutan wasn't home or this was going to be difficult. There was no way he would let us in his trailer and there was no way I was missing out on this. My love for Boyd was what had gotten me here, I owed it to him to see him off. James waited in the driveway for me to approach the front door. It was locked. I gritted my teeth in frustration.

"The back window?" he offered softly. I nodded and he followed me around the side of the trailer. I climbed in first, my eyes locked on the fiberboard cabinets, the orange linoleum floor, the dirty fridge. I waited until James was standing beside me, his warmth like a lighthouse on a stormy night. I needed him to see clearly.

I opened my eyes.

Boyd's body was lying exactly where I had first found it, but instead of something horrible, I saw something beautiful. Me. I was draped over his body like a blanket, my chest shaking as I'd gone to that place inside my head that kept me sane. It wasn't that I liked seeing myself in anguish or that Boyd's death didn't still upset me, but what I saw was love. I had loved him, still loved him, as purely and as fully as I could. I blinked back tears and took a step forward, expecting the soft squelch of the blood infused carpet to take away that feeling and make me sick. There was nothing and I was reminded that this was just a memory. It was time to retrieve Boyd.

I knelt down, my fingers trembling, and pressed the tips softly against my forehead first. It was time for me to come back, too. I'd been in a dark place for so long, I was beginning to crave the light. I moved over to Boyd next, hesitating just a moment before releasing him. The image of us faded away as if it had never been and I saw Boyd standing in what had been the circle of his blood.

A thousand words clogged in my throat and silenced me. I waited for him to turn around, anticipation tearing at my ribcage and leaving my heart open for all to see. When he finally did, his eyes opened wide and his face blanched. Even a ghost could be surprised.

"Neil?" I nodded but didn't speak. I wasn't ready for that yet. "You weren't the one that released me so I … " He trailed off. Someone else had released Boyd and sent him to the Library. It made my soul burn with jealousy, but I tried to push it back. James and I were here now. That was what really mattered. "But how did you … ?" He didn't finish the question. It hung in the air between us like a cloud.

Tell him you love, tell him you always have, tell him you're sorry for breaking his heart and let him know that he always has yours.

I parted my dry lips to speak when I heard it. The sound of a flute, soft and low, filtered into the room and wrapped its tentacles around Boyd. I screamed a warning, but it was too late. Boyd was changing in front of my eyes. His back bent sharply, his vertebrae burst from his skin like knives, sharp and glistening with blood. I stumbled forward and reached out for him. *I can't let this happen, not now.* James grabbed my arm just as the trailer began to shake beneath us.

"We'll come back for him," James mouthed. I shook my head. I wasn't leaving Boyd as a monster. I couldn't, no, *wouldn't* do it. James snatched my bag with the harp from its place on my belt, snapping the clasp, and took off towards the back window. I had no choice but to follow. The Boyd-thing was fully formed now and it was *angry.* It took off after me with a scream of rage, like shattering glass, and burst through the island in the kitchen, sending wood and hardware across the room in a spray of shrapnel.

James grabbed my arm and tugged me roughly through the window. The metal scraped my knees raw and sent us both sprawling into the grass. I sat up and slapped him in the face before I could stop myself. I hadn't meant it, James had only been trying to help me and I knew I wasn't thinking clearly, but it made me feel better. He didn't say anything, just stood up and handed me my bag. I tied it to my belt with the broken strap and knotted it twice.

Boyd was snarling at the window like something from the movie *Alien.* It singed my heart to see him like that. I reached for my harp, but James stopped me with a hand on my shoulder.

"She's here," he whispered. I turned around and found Jessica lounging by the car, a sardonic smile on her face. I twisted my fists in my sweatshirt. It was taking all of my willpower not to charge her and slap her a hundred times harder than I'd slapped James. I loved her, but I also loved Boyd. Fucking with him was not okay with me.

"Let him go, Jessica," I said calmly, trying not to panic. She didn't know about the harp yet. That was where I had the advantage. I couldn't give that away yet, not even to save Boyd, not if I could do it later. She frowned at me and her face was that kind of ugly pretty that makes movie stars famous. For a second, I almost wished she were still a demon. It would've been easier to send her on. I could've pretended that the ire in her eyes was something brought on by magic or death. I could've pretended that my sister wasn't like that, that deep down, she was still good. I closed my eyes for a moment to readjust my feelings and pulled my hood up like a blanket. I still had to believe that. I had to believe that inside of her, there was still something worth saving.

I opened my eyes and tried to pretend I had on purple lenses. I would see everything in a different color. I had to try.

Jessica glanced over at Boyd's demon, still snarling at the window, white spittle showering down like the world's worst snowstorm. James stepped away, but I stayed. It was still Boyd in there, somewhere. Jessica sliced her hand through the air like she was cutting something and Boyd went silent. He pulled back from the window and I could see the trailer grunting and adjusting as he moved around inside. Fear gripped my heart as I imagined him escaping and coming after me.

Would I be able to stand seeing Ehferea's arrow slice through his heart? I looked up at the sky for signs of the harpies, but neither had arrived yet. They wanted us to do this on our own, I got that, but I hoped they were nearby, just in case.

"Why are you doing this to me?" I'd asked her that before, but she hadn't responded. Maybe I could get her talking again so that I could understand why and I would be able to make peace with her memory. As things stood, it seemed like I was going to be traumatized by her lack of respect towards me for the rest of my life. If I could get her to talk, really talk, maybe I could get the harp out and strum it before she had a chance to sic one of her demons on me. I exchanged a look with James. His eyes told me not yet. I fingered the clasp of the purse and waited.

"Tate," Jessica laughed, low and hollow and forced. "I'm only trying to help you. You just don't seem to understand." She turned back towards the forest and whistled. The trees swayed and shook and I grasped James' hand with force. She wasn't looking. It was time. I opened the bag and grasped the harp with one hand.

A scream shattered the silence, breaking my concentration. It was Jarrod. Jessica looked over her shoulder and smiled at me.

"Come down to the grove," she said and began to disappear into the trees. "And we can start our new lives together." I pulled the harp out and strummed a string. My fingers hit the chord, but nothing happened, just a melodic spark and then nothing. I turned to James, suddenly afraid. He shook his head, eyes wide.

"The harpies," he whispered. I looked around but didn't see them. "No," he continued, his voice breaking. "The harpies are tied to the instruments, Tate. They give them their magic. If it isn't working … " I almost choked. *Dead, they were dead, too.* I turned to the side and tried to hold back my lunch.

"That might've been useful if you'd told me that before," I whispered, wondering how much else he knew about the harpies that he wasn't sharing. We had a connection with them, I could see that, but I had no idea how deep it went.

"They could just be in the Library," he suggested and reached back for something in his jeans. He didn't sound like he believed that. Another scream broke the silence of the trailer park. It was faint and it was getting fainter. Not a good sign. James and I took off in unison and ran through the darkness of the trees, down the hill and past the edge of the school wall. Jessica was way ahead of us, having ridden yet another one of her demons down to the cemetery that Grandpa and Mom and even she, had been buried in.

When we arrived, we were panting and I couldn't but wonder if I was going to burst a lung and feel rough stitches every time I breathed. I paused at the edge of the clearing and watched Jessica trace her fingers over her own headstone. At first, all I saw was her, but as my eyes adjusted, I realized that Jarrod was there, too. He was on the ground in a fetal position, his body covered in red. Blood. I tried to go to him, but James held me back, nodding his chin at the trees.

There were demons everywhere. There were white monkeys with pink eyes and horse faces. There were pigs with bushy tails and long, slender legs like deer. There were even winged lizards that flashed with color and zipped along the tree line like dragonflies. There had to be at least twenty of them, all different shapes and sizes and colors. All people who had been manipulated by my sister, the necromancer who pulled demons from their graves.

"I'm glad you decided to come willingly," she said as she picked up a vase from her own grave and threw it. The faded glass smashed into an angel, breaking into pieces that fell to the wet earth and glittered like rubies. *Jessica, don't.* My heart contracted with pain. I had placed those there for her not long ago. The disrespect she had for me was liable to break my spirit. She turned around and smiled again, like a piranha, ready to tear flesh and wound souls. "Because I thought you might want to see this."

She raised her hand and a line of darkness appeared down the center of the grass between us. It slithered into place like shadows, sparking like a power line, and snapped over Jarrod's body like a whip.

His scream cut through the forest like a knife, silencing birds, silencing the other demons, even the wind ceased to blow for a moment. Blood splattered my face and hair as I watched open mouthed. The creature that Jessica had been commanding crawled from the grass in a flash of dark lightning, flickered across the grove and smashed into me. Darkness wrapped around me and threw me forward, towards Jessica. I rolled across the grass and came up face to face with Jarrod's spirit. His eyes were wide, his mouth pleaded. I sat up and scooted away from him, watched as Jessica put the flute to her lips and played.

Jarrod shifted from a red headed boy to a streak of color, like sunlight through a prism. He wasn't an animal like some of the others but a bit of light that caught my eyes and drew them in like a stained glass window. I was enraptured and found I could barely look away.

"Tate!" It was James. The worry in his voice drew me to my feet and turned me to face him.

The dark creature had pinned him to a tree. My heart exploded in my chest. *Please no, don't hurt him.* I began to run. I don't know what I thought I could do, but I had to try. *Where's Ehferea with her bow and arrow when I need her?* I tried to forget that she'd mentioned that Jessica had a weapon that could kill her. If she were dead, Jessica would kill me and bind my spirit with her music and James … She was jealous of him. I could see it in her eyes. She might not be able to kill him, but she could hurt him. Over and over and over again.

I made it about halfway there before I was pulled to the ground by Jarrod. I tried to kick out at him, but I didn't know where to aim. My foot flew forward again and again as I was dragged back across the grass. It felt like I was finding purchase, but the blur of light that he had become was so foreign to me that I had no idea if what I was doing would deter him or just piss him off. My fingers itched to go to the harp, but I couldn't do it with Jessica's eyes boring into mine. If she found out about the harp and it didn't work, I might not get another chance.

Spirits crowded around me like one of those

paintings that Abe had liked where swarms of oni, Japanese demons, descended towards an honorable samurai. They reached out, touched me, brushed crooked fingers, featherless wings, hairless tails against my skin. Jessica's touch was in each one of them. She was in complete control.

I leaned forward, stomach muscles screaming in protest as I tried to get to the pocketknife in my boot. It might not help, but I was running out of options. I managed to grab the wooden handle with the tips of my fingers and pulled it out, only to have it snatched away from me by what I would've sworn was a capuchin monkey.

I screamed, partially from fear for myself, for James, and partially from frustration.

A whistle cut through my shouts, like missiles dropped from a jet and flashes of color exploded like fireworks across the graveyard. The light cast shadows across the gravestones and the demons throwing up shadows that would haunt me for the rest of my unlife.

Suddenly, Nethel was there, leaning down, tugging me to my feet. Jarrod was nowhere to be seen. I didn't hesitate, just reached into my purse and plucked the harp while Jessica was distracted. Still, there was nothing. I turned to the pale faced harpy and wondered angrily why she wasn't saving James. The fireworks were still exploding and I couldn't see if he was okay. It was hard not to try and rush through whatever it was that Nethel had done and try to find him.

"Last time I touched this fucking thing, I broke out into an aria. What the fuck is going on?" Nethel watched me carefully and if I wasn't mistaken, I thought her pale skin might've been whiter than usual.

"I cannot find Ehferea," she said simply. I blinked at her, trying to get rid of the sunbursts behind my eyelids. Of course, one harpy wasn't enough …

"But…" Nethel grabbed my arm suddenly and turned me to face the forest behind us.

"She is your guardian, Tatum, as I am James. It is her soul that adds magic to your harp. Find her there, among the trees. Go." She shoved me forward and when I tried to look back, she pushed me again. "Go!" It was the most emotion I had ever heard in her voice. I decided that was motivation enough. She wouldn't let anything happen to James. I had to trust that.

I moved through the forest, trying to feel that connection with my harp that I'd felt since they'd first given it to me. I could hear shouts and movement behind me. Jessica wouldn't let me leave for long. I forced myself forward through blackberry bushes that stung like bees and over a crest that was cut in half by one of the school walls.

Ehferea was propped against it like a doll, her head hanging between her knees and blood leaking down to drip from her nose to the forest floor.

I collapsed beside her, unsure if I should touch her or not.

"My apologies," she said, startling me. She raised her head slowly and smiled a gentle smile. "I might've given you your gift in place of Nethel, but I was afraid that you did not like me." It took me a moment to understand what she was talking about. The harp. I shook my head.

"It's okay," I told her, unsure of what I was

supposed to do. She was bleeding profusely from a wound in her stomach but was too hunched over for me to see it properly. She reached out a hand and touched my chin with her nails. Across her wrist was a bracelet I'd never seen before in black gold. It sparkled in the little bit of sun that managed to reach us through the trees.

"The soul tracker," she whispered. "Its magic is interfering with my ability to power the harp." I raised an eyebrow but didn't say anything about the blood. If she thought she was okay, I was going to have to trust her. In reality, I knew nothing about the harpies. "Please remove it." I slid the bracelet off of her wrist and opened my purse.

"No," she said suddenly, her eyes wide and full of pain. "Put it on and go. Jessica will not be able to track you. Approach her slowly and use your single chance wisely."

"Are you going to be okay here?" I asked, hastily slipping the bracelet on and rising to my feet. The demons were getting closer. I could practically smell them, one part anger and two parts desperation. Her eyes glittered and she nodded before letting her head hang loosely again. I bit my lip and backed away slowly. I had to trust her, too. It was hard, but maybe it was some kind of test that I'd set for myself in a past life.

I took a deep breath and followed the wall until gravestones began to dot the ground around me. The cemetery was old and trees had sprung up over the years, obscuring the oldest graves. I used them as cover as I followed the trail of death to my sister.

Unfortunately for me, she was across the field with Nethel, who was lying motionless in the grass. And James.

"Jessica, don't!" I shouted, stumbling into the clearing. Blood was soaking the front of my sweatshirt making it heavy and cumbersome to move around. She ignored me like she'd done a million times before and put the flute to her lips. It was like I could see the music streaming from the silver metal, wrapping around the gathered spirits and twisting them until they were unrecognizable. In her eyes, I saw death. James and mine both.

"Did you know?" her wicked voice had whispered *in my ear. "The only way to kill a summoner is with a knife, soaked in the blood of a loved one?"*

I pressed my hands over my head to block out the memory.

"Neil!" James was screaming at me from across the grove. I looked up at him. He was still pinned to the tree by the demon that had thrown me. I pulled my sweatshirt off and started to run. This was my fault. I'd had the chance to stop Jessica before. I could've made her transition peacefully. Instead, I'd been selfish. I was going to have to deal with the consequences of that. *Please let Boyd be okay,* I thought. *Please don't let his love for me be his undoing.*

"You don't have a choice now, Neil. Come here or I'll rip his fucking head off," she mocked as demons moved towards James, drawn like moths to light. I locked eyes with the person that had managed to become my best friend in a matter of days. He was scared but brave. His eyes told me not to move forward. *Am I in love with him?* I wondered. I'd never been in love before, but I knew the love I felt for James was different than the kind I'd felt for Abe or my mother or Boyd. I took a deep breath and used that thought as fuel to push my shaking legs forward. There was nothing I could do for Jarrod and deep down, I was glad. It was sort of his fault that we were here in the first place. Jessica had loved him wholly and utterly and he had spit on that love, turned her into this monster. She may have still looked pretty, but Jessica was the most demonic one of them all.

I checked to make sure the harp was still strapped to my belt. I had learned my lesson at the school and again, at the park. I wouldn't drop it again.

"I'm so happy, Tate," she whispered, her eyes full of tears. "You and me and Jarrod, we'll be together forever. There's nothing better than that, Tate, nothing." My fingers twitched near the strings. *She pushed you off of that cliff.* The thought didn't make what I had to do any easier. I glanced back over at James. He was okay still but for how long? Jessica had killed Jarrod without much thought. I didn't have any time to question myself.

I paused in front of her, our bloody shoes nearly toe to toe.

She pulled the knife across her wrist in one last, cruel gesture.

I pulled the first string. Music wrapped around me, lifted me up like wings and took me to that other place where the people I loved didn't die and the hurt I felt was just a distant star in the sky.

I closed my eyes and let the sound of music wash over and through me. It was the sound of Ehferea's soul singing gently, beckoning to me. My feet moved to follow her voice, my voice, entangled together in the words I'd read but hadn't understood. *She lies twist'd, twist'd twist'd.* I had been twisted, by pain, by fate, by loss, but I was starting to understand that there was more to me than that. I was starting to realize that I could untangle myself from the hurt and still be me. I could still love, I could still live. I opened my eyes and stopped. This song wasn't for me. It was for my sister, my twin, my heart.

"Tate?" Jessica whispered, looking back at me through blue eyes that sparkled with tears and confusion and fear.

"I'm here," I said and pulled her against me and then there was nothing but us. I stroked her hair back and let the harp lull us to the ground where we knelt, just the two of us, and let the hurt soak away into the grass like rain.

"I'm afraid," she said, clutching my shirt with a shaking fist. Her body shook while she cried the tears she'd been holding back for so long. I rubbed her back in little circles and tried to breathe in the scent of her hair. This was goodbye, but that was okay. She had left me before in a whirlwind of pain and misunderstanding and frustration. Now was our chance to make that right. "And I'm sorry." She pulled away from me and cupped my cheeks with her hands before planting a kiss on my forehead like she'd always done when we were little. I took her hands in my own and pulled them down, stared at identical fingers and identical knuckles wrapped together in love.

"I forgive you," I told her, my own eyes dry. I couldn't let her see me cry for her lost life. It was my turn to be strong. When Mom had died, she had shouldered the brunt of the hurt. I could do the same for her. "And I'm sorry, too, for not understanding how hurt you were. If I had seen the signs I would ... " She shushed me with a finger to my lips and stood. She was gazing away from me, at something I couldn't see. I didn't turn around, but I knew that whatever it was, it was good and that my sister would be taken care of. I watched her face sparkle. The anger was gone, the betrayal was gone. She was just Jessica again.

Her clothes fell from her body until she stood naked and full of a light I had thought she had lost. When she began to walk away, I let her. I let the music fade away into the sound of the wind against the headstones and I watched as the demons around me changed into people with smiles and frowns and tears and laughter. James fell to his knees at the base of the tree, freed from the demon's grip. I stayed there, kneeling, waiting for my heart to stop pounding.

He came to me and sat down while Ehferea and Nethel stood behind him, hurt but alive. I smiled then and that's when the tears I'd been holding back burst forth. She was gone. She was really gone this time and I had sent her away. I had done it. I had loved her and I had proved it, but God, it had hurt so much.

"James?" I said, unable to move or even breathe. He came forward, through the mud and pulled me against him, holding me while I cried for a job well done and a job that had yet to come.

It was time to say goodbye to Boyd.

James and I sat in the center of the clearing together while I let the tempestuous sea of my emotions relax into a quiet thunder. Nethel had retreated back into the forest and I knew that she would take care of Ehferea as James was taking care of me. I needed to go back and help Boyd, but first, I would take this moment for Jessica. I laid on my back in the grass and held her sweatshirt in my hands, putting the bloody fabric to my face. It still smelled like her. It wouldn't for long, but for now I was glad because it was just what I needed. James gave me a few moments for my thoughts before speaking.

"You were brave," he told me softly. I nodded but didn't speak. Losing her again was hard, but the way she'd looked at me in that last moment, that was beautiful. She'd been happy. It had been a long time since I'd seen her like that.

"I don't feel brave," I admitted. James nodded and scooted closer to me, lifting my head into his lap.

"Bravery isn't about not being scared," he told me, looking down into my eyes. I traced the new stitches over his eyebrow. "It's about pushing forward even though you are scared." I put the sweatshirt over my face. James pulled it back. "It's time to be brave again," he told me without mercy. I was stalling. I glanced away.

"I fucked it all up, James," I said, rolling onto my side. He kept my head in his lap and waited. I had to tell him now. Jessica was gone. I didn't have that as an excuse anymore. I wanted James to know before he touched Boyd that it was my fault. "He loved me so fucking much and I just wanted him to be happy. I didn't do it on purpose." James' breath sped up and I recognized that he was feeling like I'd felt at the table. He was seeing me in his own mirror. *Are we soul mates?* I wondered absently. I didn't know much about that, but I knew we were partners. Now and forever, harpies be damned. Friendship is eternal. *And this might be something more ...*

"We had sex and it meant nothing to me. Boyd, he cried." I picked at the grass and wished there were daisies so I could make a chain. Busy work helped the words come out. "I only did it once and I told him I didn't want it to be like that. I think he thought I didn't love him." I turned over so James could see my face, so he could see the face of a murderer. "But I did. He didn't know that and that's why he killed himself. Because of me." Tears stung again. I couldn't even believe it. I thought I had cried enough already. How many tears did I have left inside my soul? James surprised me by tearing up, too. He bent down and pressed his forehead against mine. I could feel his lips in my hair when he spoke.

"You're not a murderer," he said softly and thought I could hear the howls of Boyd's demon. We had to go back. It wasn't fair to Boyd. I waited for James to finish anyway. I wanted to hear this. I needed somebody to tell me this or I could never go and live that life I told myself that I wanted. Jessica had lost her way and I had to find mine, for both of us. "We loved as much anyone can ever love. That's why we're here, Neil. Because we have a gift. This isn't a punishment. We're here to help people." I nodded and he leaned back, reaching into his pocket for something. His hand retreated with a flash of silver.

I sat up quickly, bumping our foreheads painfully together and scooted back, rubbing my head.

"A harmonica?" I asked, taking it gently in my hand. This wasn't just any instrument. This was a part of James, like my harp was a part of me. On it, was a poem.

He lives twist'd, twist'd, twist'd,
Finds sol'ace at gray cliffs mist'd,

Soul is broken, blacken'd, dead,
His heart beats no more, clots with dread,

Pale and quilt'd, skin like ashe,
His eyes have darken'd, can't go back,

Lost and lonely, without hope,
Transitioner, save us, lead us home.

I think I read it four times before I looked back up at him. His eyes were raw and wanting. I handed him my harp.

"That was you?" I asked. "At the park?" The twang I had heard, the thing that had broken Jessica's music.

It had been him. He nodded but didn't speak as he read my poem. His eyes moved over the words as mine had, with understanding. We understood each other.

"I've been to the Akashic Library," he whispered quietly as the breeze played her soft fingers through his hair. He gestured at the harmonica with his chin. "I can open up a door with that. It's how I got the harpies to the park. If you want to go there later, I'd be happy to take you. It is beautiful and since Jessica's not tracking you anymore, it should be safe." A smile crept up to my lips without my knowledge and then, as surreptitiously as it had come, it morphed into laughter. James stared at me, eyes wide with surprise. I think it might've been the first time he'd heard my real laugh. It felt good, like my lungs were full of bubbles. James smiled back at me and laughed, too. It was wonderful. Things could get better. They would get better, but there was something I had to do first.

"Let's go get Boyd," I said, rising from the grass and reaching my hand out to help James up. This would hurt, of course it would, but I was going to get the chance to say goodbye. I would have the opportunity to tell Boyd how I really felt and afterward, I had something to look forward to. I had a new friend, I had love, I had purpose.

I had a life.

CHAPTER TWENTY-ONE

I played the harp again outside the trailer window and waited until the howling and the trembling had stopped. When we climbed back through, I was relieved to see that Boyd was waiting for us, standing over the spot he had died with a fond smile. I didn't understand it, but then again, it wasn't really my place. I wasn't ready to die, that much had been made quite clear to me when Jessica had held the knife above my trembling form. I shook my head. That was not how I was going to remember her. I was going to think of the love we had always shared and how in the end, that was all that had mattered.

Boyd turned and faced me, his smile softening as our eyes met.

"Hey Neil," he said. My legs shook, my lips

trembled. James reached down and scooped up one of my hands with his. *Don't be mad,* I thought at Boyd. *Don't hate me for this. I didn't mean to fall in love. I never wanted this.*

"Hey," I replied, feeling suddenly shy. I was ready for this. After seeing the bliss in Jessica's face, I knew this was right, but that didn't mean it was going to be easy. I turned to James and pitched my voice to a whisper. "Do you mind if we have a moment before – " I paused. *This is right, Neil. You know this is right.* "Before you pass him on?" James nodded and pushed my hood back so that my hair shone under the moonlight streaming in the window. He gave my hand one last squeeze and left, the trailer door swinging in the breeze.

"I've really missed you," Boyd said from behind me. I turned around slowly and searched his eyes for signs of jealousy. There wasn't any. I breathed a sigh of relief.

"I've missed you, too," I said and then I broke down, collapsed to my knees and cried. The wetness that traveled down my face wasn't the same as before. It wasn't pain and agony and hurt. This time it was just release and it felt good, like I was being purified. Boyd knelt down next to me but didn't touch me. We couldn't touch, that much had been made clear to me in the past few days. A summoner has her own crosses to bear.

"Neil," he said. "Tell me about it."

And I did.

I told him how mad I was at him, how hard he'd made life for me, how I'd died by my own sister's hands. Then I realized I was being selfish.

"What about you?" I asked. "How have you been?" A thousand emotions flickered across his green eyes before he shook his head of curly hair. *Just like my dream,* I thought. It must've been an omen though I hadn't known it until now.

"There's too much, Neil," he said and his voice was both happy and sad. "You'll understand when … " He paused as he reached a hand out and traced the line James had followed when he'd pushed my hood back. "When it's your turn." I wanted to know everything. I wanted to know if he blamed me, if he still loved me, if he regretted doing it. I nodded out of respect and rose to my feet. Boyd followed suit.

"I'll call James," I said, not wanting Boyd to leave but knowing that if I didn't do it soon, it'd be that much harder for the both of us.

"Wait," he said, looking away as if he were scared to say what he was thinking. I waited, my insides bursting with emotion. "Do you think you could take me there?" I raised an eyebrow at him. "The cliff, the beach where you died?" My heart fluttered in my chest and I smiled.

"I couldn't think of a better way for you to go."

I stood on the edge of the cliff where I'd lost my life and somehow, miraculously, gotten it back again. Boyd paused on the ledge beside me.

"You know," he said and I could hear the tears in his voice though I refused to look. If I looked at him again, I would cry, too, and I was tired of crying. It was time to celebrate a new beginning for all of us. For James, for Jessica, for Boyd. I felt a sob building in my chest. *For me.* "I never blamed you," he said and I bit my lower lip to hold my emotions back. I had been hoping he would say that. "And I can't stand the thought that you ever felt that way." I let my eyes slide over to him. He was holding the railing in one hand and gazing at the sea with cloudy eyes. There was adventure there, the need for change, the desire to move on. I glanced down at my shaking hands and for a moment, I wished that it was me and not James that would be sending Boyd on.

"Neil?" he whispered, his voice nearly torn away by the ocean breeze. I nodded to let him know I had heard him. "I love you and I always will, no matter what lifetime I find myself in." I spun around and threw my arms around him. This was it. This was perfect. Like the harpies had said, this was love. It didn't have to be romantic, it just had to be. Love was important, no matter the capacity.

I pulled back suddenly, afraid that Boyd would become a demon again and send me tumbling down the cliff. He didn't. He stood there and smiled, his body shimmering and flickering like an old movie. James stepped up beside us and I grasped his hand for support.

"I feel like I know you," James said and Boyd smiled. *Good, they don't hate each other. I couldn't stand it if they hated each other.* James took a deep breath. "Well," he continued, his eyes shifting nervously over to me. I smiled encouragement. "Are you ready?" Boyd nodded. I stepped back and wrapped my arms around myself. I had seen him go once and it was one of the worst experiences of my life. I wouldn't let it be this time.

James held out his hand, his pale fingers gray in the evening light and brushed them against Boyd's forehead.

"I love you, too," I shouted, loud enough for him to hear over the wind and the water crashing against the rocks. Boyd's face lit up like the brightest star in the sky and I found my heart slamming against my chest. It was time to let him go. His spirit had stayed around long enough trying to protect me, to make sure I'd be happy. It was his turn.

Boyd's image faded until there was nothing left of him but my memory.

James turned around and cupped my face in his hands.

"I love you, Tatum Ruby O'Neil," he said and I felt the tears I'd been holding back finally burst free. James brushed them away with the pads of his thumbs and pressed the gentlest of kisses against my lips. It was our first and most perfect kiss. "Are you going to be okay?" he asked. I leaned into him and relaxed into the feel of his arms around me. Boyd was gone, but he'd be back. In another face, in another lifetime, I'd see him and I'd know. I'd recognize that smile anywhere. It was goodbye, but it was only temporary.

"Yeah," I said, surprising myself. I had always wanted to die but now, suddenly, I was ready to live. "I am, I really am."

James released me and stepped back, offering his hand. I took it gently and entwined my fingers with his. "James," I said as we walked back towards the parking lot and the waiting harpies, who were both, luckily, still alive and well. "I love you, too." He grinned at me, stretching the stitches in his face.

"I know," he replied. "But I'm glad you said it." My chest warmed and I found myself looking forward to the future. I had always thought death was the end, the culmination of a series of mishaps and suffering, but now I knew for us, it was just the beginning.

If you enjoyed this book, look for more by C.M. Stunich!

About the Author

C.M. Stunich was raised under a cover of fog in the area known simply as Eureka, CA. A mysterious place, this strange, arboreal land nursed Caitlin's (yes, that's her name!) desire to write strange fiction novels about wicked monsters, magical trains, and Nemean Lions (Google it!). She currently enjoys drag queens, having too many cats, and tribal bellydance.

She can be reached at author@cmstunich.com and loves to hear from her readers. Ms. Stunich also wrote this biography and has no idea why she decided to refer to herself in the third person.

Happy reading and carpe diem!
www.cmstunich.com

Printed in Great Britain
by Amazon